THE PRITCHER MASS

Books by Gordon R. Dickson

THE PRITCHER MASS
THE TACTICS OF MISTAKE
DANGER—HUMAN
NONE BUT MAN
NECROMANCER
PLANET RUN (with Keith Laumer)
THE SPACE SWIMMERS
NAKED TO THE STARS
SPATIAL DELIVERY
ALIEN FROM ARCTURUS
MANKIND ON THE RUN
THE GENETIC GENERAL
DELUSION WORLD
TIME TO TELEPORT
THE ALIEN WAY
SECRET UNDER ANTARCTICA
SECRET UNDER THE CARIBBEAN
SECRET UNDER THE SEA
SPACE WINNERS
MISSON TO UNIVERSE
SPACEPAW
SOLDIER, ASK NOT
EARTHMAN'S BURDEN (with Poul Anderson)
MUTANTS
HOUR OF THE HORDE
SLEEPWALKER'S WORLD
OUTPOSTER

The Pritcher Mass

by Gordon R. Dickson

Doubleday & Company, Inc., Garden City, New York 1972

ISBN: 0-385-05669-9
Library of Congress Catalog Card Number: 72-76151
Copyright © 1972 by Gordon R. Dickson
Copyright © 1972 by The Condé Nast Publications Inc.
All Rights Reserved
Printed in the United States of America
First Edition

THE PRITCHER MASS

CHAPTER ONE

*"Late on the third day, at the very moment when,
at sunset, we were making our way through a herd of
hippopotamuses, there flashed upon my mind, unforseen
and unsought, the phrase, 'Reverence for Life.' . . .
Now I had found my way to the idea in which affirmation
of the world and ethics are contained side by side;
now I knew that the ethical acceptance of the world
and of life, together with the ideals of civilization
contained in this concept, has a foundation in thought . . ."*

Out of My Life and Thought by
Albert Schweitzer

CHAZ SANT had evoked the familiar passage from Schweitzer
out of the cluttered attic of his memory. It was to help him
do battle with the grim anger still burning inside him at having once more failed the paranormals test for work on the
Mass. If there was anything he believed in utterly, it was the
cool, clean thought the old humanitarian had laid out in that
passage; but the hot flame of his own, always too-ready, fury
was hard to put down. He knew as well as he knew his own
heartbeat, that he had the special ability to pass that test.
Only, it had been as if something was deliberately tripping
him as he took it—

A sudden shrieking of rail car brakes and a heavy pressure
of deceleration jerked him out of his thoughts. He lifted his
head, staring around. Everyone else in the packed car was

also staring around. But the brake shriek and the deceleration
went on, pressing all their upright bodies hard against the
straps of the commuter harnesses that protected them.

With a rough jolt, they stopped. There was a second of
absolute silence; then the faint but distinct sounds of two ex-
plosions from somewhere ahead of them—so faint, in fact,
that they had to come from outside the sterile seal of their
car, the middle one of a three-car Commuters Special on this
18:15 run from Chicago to the Wisconsin Dells.

Then the abnormal silence was shattered by a roar of
voices. It was a typical crowded day's-end run; and everyone
in the car's two hundred and forty harnesses seemed to be
talking at once, making guesses at what had happened. Chaz
himself was strapped in next to the long window running
along the right side of the car, but he could see nothing unusual beyond its double thicknesses of glass. Only a twilight,
autumn-brown, and weedy landscape of the unsterile outside;
a field that might once have been farmed acres but was now
rough with clumps of aspen saplings and the occasional
splash of deadly color from the golden fruit of a Job's-berry
bush.

He craned his neck, trying to see up along the track forward; but at this spot it curved to the left through a stand of
pines and there was nothing to be seen that way either only
the trees and the bulging windowed right side of the Special's
first car.

"Sabotage," said the thin woman in the harness to Chaz's
immediate left. Her face was pale except for small spots of
color over her prominent cheekbones; and her voice was tight.
"It's always on an evening run like this. The rails are going to
be torn up ahead. Our seal will get cracked, somehow; and
they'll never let us back into the Dells . . ."

She closed her eyes and began moving her lips in some silent prayer, or ritual of comfort. She looked to be in her late
thirties or early forties—pretty once, but time had been hard
on her. The atmosphere in the car stayed noisy with specu-

lations. After a minute, however, the train jerked and started
again, slowly gathering speed. As the car Chaz was in went
around the curve and emerged from the trees he got a clear
view of what had halted it, spilled on the roadbed to the right
of the steel tracks, less than twenty feet beyond the window
and himself.

The saboteur had been a man in his mid-fifties, very thin,
wearing only the cut-off trouser lower half of a jumpsuit, with
a thick, red, knit sweater. He had apparently found an old
railway speed cart somewhere—a real antique, probably from
some infected museum. The little vehicle was nothing more
than a platform and motor mounted on rail car wheels. This
had been loaded with a number of brown cardboard cartons,
possibly containing explosives. With these, he had apparently
tried to ram the train head on.

What they had heard must have been two solid-missile
shots from the computer-directed, 75-millimeter Peace cannon on the first car. One shot had missed. There was a fresh-
torn hole in the ground, five feet to the right of the tracks.
The other had knocked the wheels off one side of the speed
cart, and thrown cart, rider, and cargo off the tracks. If there
had been explosives in the cartons, they had not gone off—
probably stale. Concussion, or something like it, must have
killed the saboteur, because there was not a mark on him although he seemed obviously dead—his open eyes staring up
at the red sunset stains in the haze-thick sky, as he lay
sprawled on his back by the shattered speed cart.

He was brown-skinned and emaciated, with the red spots
of ulcers on his throat. Plainly in the last stages of Job's-berry
rot. . . .

There was a long-drawn shudder of breath from the woman
in the harness at Chaz's left. He glanced at her and saw her
face had no color in it at all now. Her eyes were open again,
staring at the dead man.

"He'll have planted something else up ahead to break us
open—I know he'll have," she said.

Chaz looked away from her uncomfortably. He could not blame anyone for fearing the rot. A single spore could slip through the smallest crack in a sealed environment, be inhaled and take root in human lungs, to grow and spread there until the one who had inhaled it died of asphyxiation. But to see someone living in a constant, morbid fear of it was something that seemed to reach inside him, take hold of a handful of his guts and twist them.

It was the sort of emotional self-torture in which his Neopuritanic aunt and cousins indulged. It had always both sickened him to see them slaves to such a fear and filled him with a terrible fury against the thing that had made slaves of them. To a certain extent, he felt the same way about all people with whom he shared this present poisoned and bottled-up world. The two conflicting reactions had made him a loner; as friendless and self-isolated as a man could be under conditions in which people were physically penned up together most of the time, as they were on this train.

He hung in his harness, watching the roadbed gravel alongside the train start to blur in the gathering darkness, as the three cars picked up speed to a normal three hundred kilometers per hour. A pair of animal eyes gleamed at him momentarily from the gloom. Animals were generally free of the rot; forty years of research had not found out why. It was dark enough outside now for the window to show him a shadowy image, pacing the rushing train like a transparent ghost, of the lighted car; and himself—jumpsuited, of average height, with the shock of straight black hair and the face that seemed to be scowling even when it was not . . .

Details of what had happened were being passed back by word of mouth through the rows of commuters ahead of him.

"The heat-monitoring screen picked him up through the trees around the curve," the man in front of the woman next to Chaz relayed to the two rows about them, "even before they could see him. But on the screen he was just about the size of a repair scooter. So they held speed, just keyed in the computer on the cannon, and waited. Sure enough, once the comp had a clear image, it identified a saboteur, fired, and knocked him out of the way."

He twisted his neck further back over his shoulder to look at the row containing Chaz and the woman.

"Someone up ahead suggested we hold a small penitential gathering for the saboteur," he said. "Anyone back here want to join in?"

"I do," said the woman. She was one of the Neopuritanics all right. Chaz shook his head at the man, who turned his own head forward again. A little later, the car attendant came pushing amongst their close ranks, vertically unwinding a roll of thin, silver, floor-to-ceiling privacy curtain; weaving it in and out among the upright shapes of the harnessed commuters to enclose those who would join in the gathering.

"Both of you here?" he asked Chaz and the woman.

"Not me," said Chaz. The attendant took the curtain back on the far side of the woman into the rows behind them, and returned a little later to bring the curtain forward around her other side; so that—in theory at least—she and Chaz now occupied separated quarters aboard the packed railway car.

Chaz hung in his harness, watching the landscape, letting his mind drift. Muffled to faintness by the sound-absorption qualities of the privacy curtain, he could hear the gathering getting under way. They had already chosen a Speaker, who was lecturing now.

". . . remembering the words of the Reverend Machael Brown, twenty-three years ago, '*You are all a generation of Jobs, in sin and pain equally deserving—therefore, if your fellow seems to suffer and not yourself, do not think he or she is more guilty than you, or you more lucky, but only that your own share and time are merely delayed. They will be coming.*' Accordingly, in this gathering, all of us here recognize and admit our guilt toward a sick and polluted Earth, acknowledging that we are no better and no different from that infected and exiled fellow human, who just now would have made us

like himself. In token of which we will now commence by
singing Job's Doggrel Hymn. Together, now—

> "The bitter fires of hell on Earth
> "Burn inward from periphery,
> "On tainted soil the world around,
> "The breeding grounds of Job's-berry.
>
> "Pray we to God of years forgot,
> "We pray to wood and stone.
> "Pray we escape from living rot.
> "Nor do we pray alone.
>
> "In Neopuritanic cell,
> "In sealèd room and city street . . ."

. . . Chaz ceased to listen. It was one way to shut out the
emotion the hymn evoked. It was not that he was less ethic-
concerned than others. In his six-by-eight-by-seven-foot condominium apartment in the Upper Dells, he had a meditation corner like everyone else; its small tray of dark, sterilized
earth hand-raked carefully, morning and evening. In addition,
however, he had a potassium ferrocyanide crystal, growing in
nutrient solution, in a flask on the tray. Each morning, and
evening as well, he spent a half hour seated in front of that
crystal in meditative concentration. But his particular concern during these times was not world-sin; or that he be lucky
in avoiding an accident that could expose him to the rot. He
meditated with the spiritual grunt and sweat of a man digging a ditch.

He concentrated to develop whatever talent he had for
Heisenbergian chain-perception, so that he could pass the
test for work on the Pritcher Mass. So he could at last get a
chance to do something about the situation that had cowed
and was pushing to extinction his huddled people. The idea
of humbly accepting his share of humanity's sins had never

worked for him. He was built to fight back, even if the fight was hopeless.

If there was indeed such a thing as the chain-perception talent, he had decided some time ago, he was going to produce it in himself. And in fact, he felt that he now had. But for some reason he could not seem to make it operate during an examination for work on the Mass. This afternoon he had failed for the sixth time; and it had been a simple test. The examiner had spilled a hundred grains of rice, each dyed in one of five different colors, on a table in front of him, and given him achromatic glasses to put on.

With the glasses on, the grains had all become one solid, uniform gray—together with the desk, the room, and Mr. Alex Waka, the examiner. Waka had hidden the grains for a second with a sheet of cardboard while he stirred them about. Then he had taken the cardboard away, leaving Chaz to see if he could separate out all the grains of any one color.

Chaz had worked, lining up the grains he selected, so that it would be possible to know afterward where he had gone right, or wrong. But when he took the glasses off he had had only seventeen of the twenty red-colored grains in line before him. Of the last three grains he had selected, the first two were blue, the last yellow. Strong evidence of paranormal talent—but not proof.

"Damn it!" Chaz had snapped, as close to losing his temper as he ever let himself come nowadays. "I could feel something getting in my way on those last three choices."

Waka nodded.

"No doubt. I don't doubt you feel you did," he answered, sweeping the colored grains back into their box. He was a small, round-bodied man, dressed in a sand-brown jumpsuit, a three-inch fringe haircut drooping over the low forehead of his round face. "All really potential Pritcher Mass workers seem to be self-convinced of their own talent. But a demonstration of it is what we need; and a demonstration is the one thing you haven't given me."

"How about a catalyst, Mr. Waka?" Chaz asked bluntly.

Waka shrugged.

"A lot of hokum, as far as I know," he said. "About as useful as a rabbit's foot, or a lucky charm—a psychological prop but no paranormal talent stimulant."

He looked keenly at Chaz.

"What makes you think something like that might help you?"

"A theory," said Chaz, slowly. "Have you ever heard of the species-mind idea?"

"The notion of some sort of collective unconscious, or subconscious, for the human race?" Waka frowned. "That's a cult thing, isn't it?"

"Maybe," said Chaz. "But tell me something else; have you ever grown crystals in a nutrient solution?"

Waka shook his head.

"You start out with a seed crystal," Chaz explained, "and this grows by drawing on the saturated chemical solution in which it's immersed—a solution of the same chemical composition as the seed crystal. You have to keep your solution saturated, of course, but eventually your seed crystal grows many times over."

"What about it?" Waka asked.

"Assuming there is some sort of collective unconscious— or even that I just think there's a collective unconscious to draw on," Chaz said. "Then suppose I get a catalyst and can convince myself it acts like a seed crystal for my paranormal talents, which accrete around it, drawing on the nutrient solution of the collective unconscious of the mass-mind? Would it help?"

Waka shook his head.

"You have to believe you can make your talents work," he said. "That's all I know. If this, or a rabbit's foot, or anything can help you believe, then it's going to increase your apparent talents. Only—" His eyes became keen on Chaz. "As I understand it, the catalyst has to be from outside. Unsterile—and illegal."

Chaz shrugged. He carefully did not answer. He did not have a catalyst yet, in fact; or even one in prospect. But he was curious to hear Waka's reaction to the idea of his making use of something that could get him exiled from the sterile areas if it was found in his posession—in effect, condemned to death—since exposure to the outside meant death from the rot in a few months.

"Well," said Waka, after a moment's wait—and his voice changed—"let me tell you something. I believe in the salvation of humanity by one means, and one means only. That's the Pritcher Mass: which is one day going to help us transport a pure and untainted seed community of men and women to some new, clean world; so that the human race can start all over again, free from rot, spiritual as well as physical."

He paused. For a moment, he had shed a great deal of the insignificance of his tubby person and foolish haircut; and the pure light of the fanatic shone through.

"That means," he said, returning to his normal manner and tone of voice, "that as far as I'm concerned, my duty to the Mass overrides any other duty I may have, including those to purely local laws. I would not report an examinee using an unsterile object as catalyst. Am I clear?"

"You're clear," Chaz answered. His opinion of Waka had just gone up a notch or two. But he was still wary of the examiner.

"All right," Waka said, standing up behind his desk. "Then that's that for the present. Anytime you feel you can demonstrate the necessary level of talent, call me. Night or day, at any hour. Otherwise, please remember that, like all examiners for the Mass, I've got a heavy office schedule with other people just as eager as you are to go to work out beyond Pluto's orbit. Good afternoon, then. . . . May forgiveness be yours."

"Good afternoon," said Chaz.

That was that, he thought, now hanging in his train-car

harness. Give him a chance at a possible catalyst, and he certainly would not pass it up. As for telling Waka about such a catalyst, in spite of the examiner's hint that he would be on Chaz's side against the law in that case, that was something that still required thinking about—

Without warning, the world seemed to tilt under him. Train, car, fellow-commuters, everything, seemed to fly off at an angle as a terrific pressure robbed him of breath and consciousness at once.

He woke to the painful feeling that something hard was digging into the middle ribs on his right side and something rough was pressing against his left elbow. He tried to move away from whatever was digging into his ribs and above him there was a snapping sound. He fell flat, face down on more of the rough surface that had been pressing against his left elbow.

His head clearing, he became aware that he lay under something dark on what felt like a bed of small rocks. A cold, fresh current of air, laden with outdoor smells, chilled his face. Off to his right there was a variable light source and sounds of voices.

There were other sounds of voices around and above him, in the overhanging darkness. Some made sense, but most were merely the noises of people in pain and shock. Lifting his head, he saw shapes lumped about him, some making noises and some not.

"They'll never let us in the Dells again," said a toneless voice almost in his ear. "Never."

It was not memory speaking, but a live and present person. He lifted himself on his hands and looked to his left, farther into the shadow beneath the overhang. Someone was seated there, as if before an altar, legs crossed; and by her voice it was the woman who had occupied the harness next to him.

He looked in the other direction and forgot her. Suddenly, everything he saw lost its reasonless, separate identity and made sense. The dark shape hanging over him was the railway car he had been in. It had fallen half on its side and broken open, spilling him out along with some of the other commuters.

He crawled clear of the overhang and sat up. A broken part of his harness still circled his chest. He unbuckled it and let it fall. His head felt hot. The shape of a rock from the railroad ballast was cold under his left hand. He lifted it and laid its coolness against his forehead. The little relief of that touch brought his mind all the way back into reality.

He was outside, and it was night. The saboteur—or another —had indeed set a second trap for the train, farther down the track. If this was in fact the work of the saboteur they had encountered earlier, then his head-on drive at the first car had probably been to reassure the train commander that there was nothing else to fear farther up the line. But how or why the train was wrecked did not matter so much now. What mattered was that the car Chaz was in had broken open.

He was *outside*.

He was exposed to the rot, potentially infected. According to law, neither he nor any of the other commuters in that particular car would be allowed back into a sterile area again.

Oh yes, he would.

The grim refusal to accept what had happened to him exploded instinctively inside him. He was bound for the Pritcher Mass, not doomed to wander a desolated world until he died of starvation or choked on the feathery white fungus growing inside his lungs. In this one case—his own—the inevitable must not be allowed to happen.

He took the rock from his forehead, about to toss it aside —then something stayed his hand. In the flickering light that he now saw come from the burning engine section of the first car, which now lay on its side, he looked at the rock; and a word came into his mind.

Catalyst.

This was his chance, if he wanted to take it. A Heisenber-

gian catalyst, reportedly, was most often something just like
this. A piece of wood or stone, not different from any other;
illegal only because it was from an unsterilized area such as
this was. But it was the unsterilized catalysts that were supposed to be the only really effective ones.

Was his talent now telling him that what he held was such
a catalyst—the catalyst he needed to demonstrate the talent?

His fingers clamped on the stone. He half closed his eyes
against the light of the flames forty feet away and forced his
mind into channels of choice.

Chain-perception—a linked series of optimal choices
among the alternates immediately available, leading to a desired end or result. His present desired end or result was simply to get back into a sealed section of the train without anyone finding out that he had been exposed to the rot-infected
outer world. He held the rock tightly, searching about in his
mind for the next immediate action that would *feel* as if it
would lead him eventually to a safe return to the train.

He stared at the flames. A heavy cargo rescue copter was
already on the scene, down on the ground a dozen yards from
the tipped-over first car. Figures in bulky sterile suits were
attaching wide, pipe-like sections together into a sterile escape tunnel between the copter and the rooftop airlock on
the first car, the only lock available now that the car was on
its side. Each of two suited figures carried a section between
them. As Chaz watched, another cargo copter settled to the
ground by the third car and escape-tunnel sections began to
emerge there. It was only the second car then that had lost
its seal, and the passengers of which would be left to starve or
rot.

He felt the rough outlines of the rock biting into his palm
and his fingers quivered about it. Hold on and make it work,
he told himself. Hold . . . he reached out his other hand, out
to his left, and his fingers brushed against something soft and
cloth-like, warm and in some way comforting. The sleeve of
the woman who had been in the harness beside him.

Abruptly, like a shudder passing through him, came his memory of how she had feared the rot—of how she had feared exactly what had just happened here. She had been exaggerating, of course. The odds were that she, or he, or any of them, would have to spend some days in the open before they would actually inhale rot spores. But probably she would not even try to make use of what little life remained to her. From what he knew of people like her, she would simply sit waiting for death.

The terrible double feeling of disgust and pity came back on him; but pity this time was stronger. He could not leave her here to die, just like that. If the catalyst and chain-perception could get him safely back into sterile surroundings without it being suspected he had been outside, it could do as much for her and him, together.

Immediately he had made the decision, it *felt* right in terms of the logic chain-perception. Two was for some reason a good number. He leaned toward the woman and closed his hand on the slack of her sleeve.

He pulled, gently. Her murmuring, which had been going on continually all this time, broke off. For a second nothing happened, then she came toward him. Hardly thinking beyond what seemed to be the reflexes and feelings prompting him, he moved further away from the car, getting to his feet and drawing her after him.

She came like someone in a trance. They stood, both on their feet and together in the night, a little way from the broken second car, with its sounds of despairing and injured people.

Still gripping the stone in one hand and her sleeve in the other, he looked again at the sterile-suited figures outlined by the flames of the first car. The figures carried the sections with one section between each pair of them. He turned and looked at the suited figures starting to emerge from the copter opposite the last car. They also carried sections, two figures to a section.

Two—of course! That was why this series had begun with him first touching, then holding, the woman. He needed someone to help him in this chain of actions.

A feeling of certainty warmed within him. He seemed to feel the linked alternate choices that would bring both of them back to safety. He imagined these choices visible like the edges of a slightly spread stack of cards. The optimal choices of an infinite series of alternates, leading to an inevitable conclusion.

"Come on," he said to the woman. He moved off, towing her after him; and she followed like a young child after a parent.

CHAPTER TWO

He led her toward the flames and the first car. Now that he had perceived the direction in which his actions tended, he thought he would have preferred to have tried to get into the last car where there was no fire to light the scene. However, evidently his perceptions knew better. Keyed to a high emotional pitch now, he felt clearly that it was the first car rather than the last to which they should go.

Hidden in the further dark he came close to a pair of figures positioning one of the sections. It was this particular pair to which his perceptions had drawn him; and a moment later the perceptions justified their choice, as the two figures moved close together to seal one end of their section to the next—at the moment when the two working on the next section had already finished their work and headed back toward the copter.

Chaz let go of the woman and moved up softly behind the two figures. For a second, standing just behind them, he hesi-

tated. They were human beings like himself, also human beings on a rescue mission. Then he remembered that these two
would consider it their duty to shoot him on sight—and
would, with the weapons belted to their suits now for that
purpose—if they suspected him of having been one of those
exposed to the unsterilized outer environment. It was hard to
think like an outlaw. But an outlaw he was now, as much as
the saboteur who had wrecked the train.

He stood behind the two and swung the rock overhand,
twice. It gave him a hollow feeling inside to see how easily
the figures folded to the ground. One by one he dragged them
away from the tube and the light of the flames, to where the
woman still stood.

She was stirring now, coming out of her shock. It was too
dark to see her face except as a gray blur, but she spoke to
him.

"What is it . . . ?" she said. "How . . . ?"

Chaz bent over one of the figures and with fumbling haste
began to unseal the closure down the front of the suit.

"Get into one of these!" he told her. She hesitated. "Get
moving! Do you want to see the Dells again, or don't you?"

The magic effect of the last phrase seemed to reach her.
She bent over the other figure and Chaz heard the faint rasp
of the seal on its suit being peeled open.

He forgot her for a moment and concentrated on getting
into the suit of the limp body at his own feet. He got it off
and struggled into it, first tucking his catalyst stone into a
pocket of his jumpsuit. Luckily, these sterile suits were all-
sized; expandable and contractable, variable in arm and leg
length. Standing with it on at last, and resealing the closure,
he looked once more at the woman and saw she was just stepping into her own suit.

He waited impatiently until she was in and sealed. Then,
by gestures, he had her help him drag the two still-unmoving
forms back toward the tube. The tube was completed now,
and one suited figure was standing farther down by the air-

lock entrance in its middle section, checking in the other figures who were lined up ready to enter. Leaving the two they
had deprived of their suits, Chaz took the arm of the woman
and led her circuitously through darkness. They joined the
line. It moved slowly forward; and a minute later they, too,
filed through the tube airlock. Behind them, the suited figure
who had been checking the others in entered and sealed the
inner airlock door.

The other figures were now heading down the tube toward the first railway car. Chaz pushed the woman in her suit
ahead of him and followed them. Around them, there was the
hissing sound of sterilizing gas being pumped in. It would
clean not only the interior of the tube, but the exteriors of
their suits—in fact, destroying any rot spores they had not actually ingested. The hissing ceased before they caught up
with the figures at the end of the tube.

The other figures were standing, waiting, by the roof airlock of the railway car. After a second, there was the distant
whir of fans sucking out the gas, then the lighting tubes in the
ceiling of the tunnel blinked twice. Two figures next to the
airlock began working with it; and to the creak of metal
hinges not recently used, it was swung open.

The inner airlock door took a moment longer to open.
Then it, too, yawned wide and the figures began to disappear
into the dark interior of the car.

Within, the lights of the car were out. It was a horizontal
pit of darkness, filled with moans and crying. The suited figures turned on the head lamps of their helmets.

"*Limpet lights!*" roared a powerful voice abruptly in Chaz's
ears. He started, before realizing that it was the suit intercom he was hearing. There was a pause, but the darkness
persisted. The voice came again. "*For God's sake, didn't
anyone think to bring limpets? First team back bring half a
dozen and stick them around the walls in here. We need
lights! All right, let the ones who can walk find their own way
out; look for whoever's pinned, hurt, or can't walk.*"

The woman had turned her head lamp on in automatic re-
flex to seeing the lamps go on around her. Chaz reached up to
his own helmet, fumbled with thick-gloved fingers, found a
toggle by the lamp lens and pushed it. It moved sideways
and a beam of light revealed a tangle of harnesses and bodies
before him. He reached out, took the glove of the woman
again, and started pushing through the tangle toward the rear
of the car with her in tow.

They moved until, turning his head, he saw that they were
safely screened by the passengers around them from the other
suited figures. Then Chaz looked about, playing his helmet
light on the crying, struggling mass of passengers.

"All right, all right! Get them moving!" boomed the voice
over the intercom on his eardrums.

A small man, apparently unhurt and free of his harness,
was among those worming their way toward the open airlock behind Chaz and the woman. Chaz barred his way.

"Lie down," Chaz said, and then realized that even if his
voice was somehow coming through the suit's outside
speaker, it could not have been heard by the man in this
bedlam.

Chaz made motions to the other man and moved around
him, taking him by the shoulders. He waved to the woman to
take the man's feet. The woman's bulky-suited figure only
stood staring at him. Angrily, Chaz gestured; and at last she
stooped and picked up the feet. Together, clumsily, they carried the man from the car into the tube.

He had struggled slightly at first on being picked up, then
quieted and hung limp and heavy in their grasp. They
sweated with him through the crowd to the airlock and into
the tube. It was surprisingly empty. The injured near the airlock were blocking the way for those further back who could
have walked out under their own power.

Chaz and the woman carried the man down the tube. As
they approached the airlock through which they had entered,

Chaz stopped and motioned to the woman to put the feet of their burden down.

It took her a moment to understand him, as it had taken her a moment to understand that she was to help pick the man up. Then, she obeyed. Chaz lifted the man upright and gave him a push toward the copter end of the tube. He did not seem to understand at first, any more than the woman had. He stared at them for a second, then tottered off in the direction Chaz had indicated.

The tube about them was empty except for one limping, older man who hardly looked at them as he passed. Chaz let him by, then opened the inner door of the tube airlock and stepped into the lock itself. He motioned the woman in behind him, then closed the inner door on them both.

He took hold of the top end of the seal to his suit and started to take it off; but his fingers hesitated. There was a feeling inside him. Not a perceptive feeling of the sort that had brought him this far, but simply an emotional reluctance to leave the two men he had struck outside, to rot and die as he might have rotted and died.

He let go of the seal strip, waved back the woman when she started to accompany him, and opened the outer door of the airlock. The two he had hit were not hard to find. One was now sitting up, dazed, the other was evidently still unconscious.

Chaz helped the dazed one to his feet, took him back through the airlock, and pushed him into the corridor, aiming him toward the copter end of the tube. The man stumbled off like a zombie. Chaz went back and dragged the other's limp figure into the lock. With the woman's help, he shoved the man into the tube during a moment when no one else was about, then closed the inner door again and began taking off his suit.

The woman imitated him. As soon as they were out of their suits, Chaz once more opened the inner door of the lock a crack and peered out. The man they had carried in from outside was gone.

There were no suited figures in view, but the tube was now full of walking refugees from the first car. None of them paid any attention to Chaz and the woman. Boldly, Chaz led the way out into the crowd that now thronged the tube and turned to seal the airlock inner door behind them. They followed the others about them into the copter, where attendants were ushering those unhurt through a room with cots into another filled with regular airbus seats, four abreast on either side of an aisle. The walking refugees from the train were being seated and strapped in.

Chaz stepped back from the woman, pushing her away when she tried automatically to follow him.

"Forget you ever saw me!" he whispered harshly to her, and faded back into the crowd. As he was being strapped into a seat, he saw her ushered to one some three rows ahead of him, on the opposite side of the aisle.

Moments later, a white-suited attendant came by with a clipboard. Chaz slipped his hand into the pocket holding the stone and grasped it tightly.

"Name?" the attendant asked.

Chaz had to clear his throat before he could speak.

"Charles Roumi Sant," he said.

"Address?"

"Wisconsin Dells, Upper Dells 4J537, Bayfors Condominium 131, apt 1909."

"Good." The attendant noted it. "Was anyone with you on the train?"

Chaz shook his head.

"Do you see anyone here you recognize from the car you were in?"

Chaz's heart beat heavily but steadily. He hesitated, gripping the stone in his pocket. Silence was bad. A negative answer was even more dangerous, in case of a later checkup on the rescued passengers.

"There, I think," he said, nodding toward the woman. "That lady there, three up and two to the left."

"Right." The attendant wrote and passed on. Later, Chaz saw him talking to the woman and her head turn slightly, directing the attendant's gaze back toward him. The attendant looked at him, glanced at his clipboard, and told her something, then moved ahead.

Chaz sank back into his seat. Clearly, she had also had the sense to identify him as someone she had seen in the first car, thereby confirming his own story. With luck—he rubbed his fingers over the stone—there would be no more checking, and his name and hers would be buried in the list of those off the first car. But even in the case of a checkup, there was now a report he had been seen in the first car. Even if that car had been completely filled, as the second had, dead bodies were never removed; and a head count of survivors should not show any extra passengers.

"Hot chocolate, sir?"

"Attendants were going up and down the aisle now, offering hot drinks. Like most of those about him, Chaz accepted one. It was an unusually rich, real-tasting drink that might have been made with actual chocolate. He sat sipping it, letting relief flow through him with the warmth of the liquid. The stone bulked hard in his pocket and a little fire of triumph burned inside of him. The woman dared not talk and neither of the suited workers had had a chance to see the faces of either the woman or himself. After a while the copter took off and about that time, unexpectedly, he feel asleep.

He woke with a start to find the copter already landed at Central Terminal, Wisconsin Dells. It took him a few seconds to remember what he was doing in the aircraft, and when memory did return it brought first incredulity, then alarm. There could have been a sedative in the hot chocolate. If he had been searched while he was unconscious—he clutched hastily at the pocket of his jumpsuit and the hard shape of the rock reassured him. He glanced around for the

woman, but could not see her. Most of the other passengers
were already up out of their seats and crowding the aisle on
their way out.

He joined them, left the copter, and went down two levels
to the personal transit system. An area had been roped off
for the survivors of the train wreck and they did not have to
wait for cars. He got one almost immediately and programmed it for his condominium in the Upper Dells.

Five minutes later he was in the sub-basement lobby of the
condominium.

He had hoped to get quietly to his room on the nineteenth
level. In spite of his sleep on the copter he felt as if he had
just put in a non-stop, forty-eight-hour day. But a fellow
apartment owner was checking her delivery box in the lobby
and recognized him. It was Mrs. Alma Doxeil, a stern, tall,
fat woman—one of the condominium party-organizers. "Mr.
Sant!" she called. "We heard about the eighteen-fifteen wreck
on the news. Were you—"

Chaz nodded, ducking into an elevator tube that had a
platform rising by at the moment. The platform carried him
up and away from the continuing sound of her voice.

"Pray penitent, Mr. Sant. Pray pen—"

He reached the nineteenth level and was glad to see that
nowhere up and down the narrow, silver-carpeted corridor
was anyone in sight. He went hastily to his apartment, stuck
his thumb in the lock, and strode in, as the apt-comp recognized his print and opened the door. He was two strides
inside and the door had clicked closed again behind him,
when he saw he was not alone. A girl in a sand-green, tweed
jumpsuit was seated in lotus position facing the red crystal
on the tray in his meditation corner. She turned her head
sharply at the sound of his entrance and he saw that her face
was drawn and her eyes reddened.

For a moment he could not place her. Then he remembered. She was another neighbor, from the sixteenth level.
They had met at one of Mrs. Doxeil's gatherings in the con-

dominium party rooms, several months ago—a long evening, the later hours of which had been more than a little blurred as far as Chaz was concerned. His imperfect memory the next morning had been that this particular girl had not shared his blurriness and had even given him to understand that she found it more than a little disgusting in him to be that drunk.

Which did not explain how she happened to be here now in his locked apartment when he himself was away from home. He stared at her, baffled. Then understanding broke through.

"Did I key the lock to your print, that night?" he asked.

She scrambled to her feet and turned to face him. She was a tall girl—he remembered that now—gray-eyed, with long brown hair and a soft gentle face. Not pretty, not beautiful—attractive, in a way that neither of those two words fitted.

"Yes," she said. "You wouldn't go in unless I let you key it in. I just let you key it to get you to give up and lie down."

"You didn't"—he hesitated—"stay?"

"No." She shook her head.

He stood staring at her, knowing what he wanted to ask her but trying to think of some polite way of phrasing it. She solved the problem for him.

"I suppose you wonder what I'm doing here now," she said. "I've never been here since that night."

"That's what I was wondering," he said.

"The news of the train wreck was on the cube," she said. "A lot of people knew it was the train you take. I thought maybe it would help if I meditated here, at your own corner, for you." She tossed her hair back on her shoulders. "That's all."

"I see," Chaz said.

Without thinking, he slid his hand into his jumpsuit pocket and brought it out holding the stone. He stepped past her to place it on the tray of sterilized earth next to the flask with the crystal. He turned back to face her; and only then realized how odd it must look—what he had just done.

"I was bringing it home . . ." he said. He looked more closely at her face and eyes. "But it's strange. I mean you being here, meditating—"

He broke off, suddenly aware he was talking his way into dangerous areas.

"And you being one of the lucky people to live through the wreck behind sealed doors?" she asked. "Why? Or don't you believe in the aid of meditation?"

"It's not that," he said, slowly. "I'm trying to see the interlock—perceive the chain of connection."

"Oh?" She sounded both relieved and a little annoyed, for no reason he could imagine. "That's right, of course, it's that Heisenberg perceptive ability you're so concerned with. The one that can qualify you to work on the Pritcher Mass. The one that drives you to drink."

"It doesn't drive me to drink!" he said; and then, hearing the anger in his voice, he wondered why the way she put things should stir him up. "Sometimes I build up a sort of charge—you wouldn't understand. There's no use my explaining."

"No, I don't understand!" She sounded as stirred up as he was. "But I don't see why that should stop you from explaining. In fact, you—"

She checked herself and bit her lip. He stared at her curiously.

"I don't understand—" he began, but the sound of the door-call interrupted him with its soft chime. "Excuse me."

He went to the door and opened it. Outside was the woman from the train.

He stared at her, for a second stopped dead by the shock of seeing her here.

She had somehow found time to change her jumpsuit—it was not impossible that she had stepped into a store on the way here and bought a new one. At any rate, the one she wore now was a gray-pink color—an almost startling shade compared to the usual browns, grays, and blacks most people wore; and above it she had even touched up her face with artificial coloring.

She smiled at him.

"We ought to have a talk," she said. "You see, I saw you with the stone; and you still have it, don't you?"

She walked forward past him through the door.

"Yes, I can see it there in your med-corner," she said. "You and I have a lot in common—"

She broke off, staring at the girl from three levels down. Her face stayed fixed in that stare; and abruptly the artificial color on it seemed to stand out, garish and unnatural.

Hastily, Chaz closed the door and swung around to face her.

"Are you crazy?" he said. "We shouldn't be seen together. Don't you understand that?"

Still staring at the girl, she answered him.

"I understand you carried away an unsterile object from the wreck," she said, flat-voiced. "I got your name from the man who checked us, on the copter. But you don't know who I am, or anything about me. I can inform on you, any time."

"You'd be informing on yourself at the same time!" he said.

"I don't have anything unsterile that's been brought in from outside," she said. "An anonymous phone call is all it'd take for you. Even if you throw that stone away this minute, the police could find traces of its having been here."

"Oh?" Chaz said grimly. "Maybe not. What's it matter to you anyway? I saved your life—isn't that enough for you?"

"No." Now she did look at him. "My life was nothing to write home about, anyway. And for all I know I'm infected with rot right now."

"Don't be crazy!" he said. Once more, he remembered her on the train before it had been wrecked, remembered her almost sick fear of being exposed. "We were only exposed to the outside for a matter of minutes. The odds are a million to one against any infection."

"There's still that chance," she said. "That's why no one ever gets let back in once they've been exposed. With my luck, I've probably got it. You've probably got it, too." She looked once more at the girl. "I suppose you've already infected her."

"Of course not! What're you talking about? What do you want, anyway?" he exploded.

Her eyes came back to him.

"My husband died when we were both twenty-two," she said. "I was left with twins and a new baby. Three children. With ten women to every seven men, who wants a widow with three children? I couldn't even qualify for a job. I had to sit home on basic income and bring my family up. Now my kids are in their teens and they don't care about me. If I'm going to die from the rot in a few weeks, I want some little taste out of life."

She stared directly at him.

"You've got a job, and extra income," she said. "I want everything you can give me." She looked for a last time at the girl. "I was going to suggest something like a partnership; but I see now that wouldn't work."

She turned around and went to the door.

"I'll call you," she said. "And you better answer the call after you get it, if I don't catch you in. I've got nothing to lose."

She opened the door and went out. It clicked closed behind her. Out of the corner of his eye, Chaz saw the girl also moving toward the door.

"Wait!" he said, desperately, putting out a hand to stop her. "Wait. Please don't go—"

Then the walls seemed to move in on him, inexorably, and he went spinning off into unconsciousness.

CHAPTER THREE

CHAZ WAS HAVING a curious, feverish sort of dream. He was
dreaming that the Pritcher Mass was not away out beyond
Pluto, but right here on Earth. In fact he had already been at
work on the Mass, using his catalyst; and he had startled all
the other workers on it with his ability. Already he had made
contact with a possible habitable world in a system under a
GO star, a hundred and thirty light years distant. Projecting
his consciousness outward from the Mass to that world, he
had arrived mentally in an alien city of cartoon-type towers
and roadways all leaning at crazy angles. Great snails slid
along the roadways, on a thin film of flowing water that
clung to every surface, vertical as well as horizontal. An insectile alien like a seven-foot-tall praying mantis had met him
and they were talking.

". . . You've got an obligation to answer me," Chaz was
arguing.

"Perhaps," said the Mantis. "The fact remains that you're pretty tough-minded. Aggressive."

"You change schools every three or four months all the time you're growing up," said Chaz angrily—it was the sort of thing his cousins were always throwing at him—"and you'll be tough, too. You know what it's like to fight your way through a fresh roomful of kids every few months? My father was a construction engineer and he was always moving from one job to the next—"

"That's not the point," said the Mantis. "The point is, where do you go from here? Think before you answer."

"I know that one," said Chaz. "There's no limit, of course."

"There are very definite limits," replied the Mantis . . .

. . . Consciousness returned. Opening his eyes, Chaz found himself back in his own apartment. He felt clear-headed again, but utterly weak and listless. For a long moment he was puzzled by his view of the room; and then he realized he was staring at its ceiling. He was lying on the floor with his head on the knees of the brown-haired girl. She knelt, supporting his head, her own face bending over him and her long hair falling about her face and his like a privacy curtain. She was stroking his head and singing to herself, so softly he could hardly hear, some nonsense song.

"*Gaest thou down tae Chicago, sae fair?*
"*Harp at ye, carp at ye, water and wine.*
"*Thinkst thou my name but once thou art there,*
"*So shalt thou be a true love o' mine.*

"*Bid'st me I'll build thee a cradle o' withys*
"*Harp at ye, carp at ye . . ."*

Music and words had a faintly familiar ring, although the words were not the same as those he had heard with that tune before.

"Of course," he said, speaking out loud unthinkingly. " 'Scarborough Fair.' The spell-song!"

She stopped singing immediately, staring down at him. He got a feeling that he had said the wrong thing, somehow shattering an important moment.

"Is that what it is?" she said in an odd voice. "It's just an old song my mother used to sing. You folded up, all of a sudden. I . . . didn't know what else to do."

"It's a mnemonic," he said. "That was the way medieval so-called witches used to remember the ingredients for a love potion. Parsley, sage, rosemary. . . . Wait a minute—" he interrupted himself. "But that wasn't the way you sang it."

"It's only a song," she said. "I didn't know it meant anything. I just had to do something. Are you hurt?"

More concern sounded in her last three words than she might have intended, because she looked away from him as soon as she said it. He felt a tremendous desire not to move at all; but just to keep on lying where he was and let everything else—the sterile areas, the unsterile land, even the Pritcher Mass itself, all go to hell. But, of course, things were not that simple.

With an effort he sat up.

"Hurt?" he said. "No."

He got to his feet. She got to hers.

"You know," he said. "Forgive me . . . but I don't seem to be able to remember your name."

"Eileen," she said. "Eileen Mortvain. You're in trouble, aren't you?"

He opened his mouth to deny it—but she had been standing here all the time he had been talking to the woman from the train.

"It looks like it," he said.

"You actually were . . . outside? In the train wreck?"

He nodded.

"So maybe she's right—I've already infected you," he said.

"Oh, no." Her answer was quick. "You couldn't—but that woman can make trouble for you."

"I suppose," he said, grimly.

Eileen said nothing, only stood looking at him as if she was waiting for something. He stared back curiously for a moment; and then forgot her, as he remembered the catalyst. He turned back to the corner and picked it up. With it in his hand he felt more sure; and he began to think clearly.

"I'd probably better get out of here," he said.

"I'll help you," said Eileen.

He stared at her again.

"Why?"

She did not color or hesitate; but he got the feeling—perhaps it was something the catalyst had stimulated in him—that the question embarrassed her.

"You're too valuable to be thrown away just because of someone like her," Eileen said. "You're going to do something out on the Pritcher Mass that'll help the human race."

"How do you know?"

"You don't remember?" she said. "You talked to me about it for three hours down in the amusement area, that night of the party; and for nearly an hour up here, standing outside your apt door, before I could get you to go in and go to bed."

The ghost of a memory troubled the back of Chaz's mind. For a moment he almost remembered.

"That's right," he said, frowning. "We sat in the corner booth near the swimming pool; and you kept handing me drinks—"

"You got your own drinks—too many of them!" she said, swiftly. "Anyway . . . you told me what it was you hoped to do out on the Mass, when you got there. That's why I was in here praying for you, just now. I didn't want to see you wasted after what you said you'd planned to do on the Mass."

"Planned?" he said. "I'm only trying to get on the staff out there, because it's someplace things are happening—not like here on Earth."

She looked at him brilliantly, but did not answer. He gave the matter up, turning to the drawers of his built-in dresser and opening them one by one to get a small personal article that could be stuffed in the pocket of a jumpsuit. Clothes and toilet articles were no problem. He could pick those up as he needed them in any twenty-four-hour store.

"Maybe if she comes back a few times," he said, "and finds me gone, she'll give up. It's worth the chance, anyway."

He finished stuffing his pockets, turned and opened the door to the apartment.

"Here we go," he said, ushering Eileen out into the corridor and following her. He closed the door behind him, then turned to face her, suddenly feeling a little awkward. "Well . . . good-by. And thanks for thinking of me, when you heard about the train wreck."

"Not good-by," she said. "I told you I was going to help you. Where do you think you'll go now?"

"I'll get a P.R.T. car and make up my mind as I go."

"And what if she's already gone to the police?" Eileen answered. "The police can check and find the record of your credit card. Every credit card used on the Personal Rapid Transit is recorded, you know that!"

"Then I'll walk to the nearest auto-hire—" He broke off.

"Then you'll have to use your credit card there, too, won't you? You can't rent a u-drive without a credit charge," she said. "There's no regular way you can get out of the Dells without leaving a trail of credit records for the main computer. I tell you, let me help you. I can get you out another way."

He gazed at her for a long moment.

"All right," he said. "What kind of route have you got up your sleeve?"

"I'll show you," she said. "We'll need help, though. Come down to my apt, first."

He followed her as they took an elevator disk down to her level. She led the way to an apartment door and pressed her right thumb on the sensitized plate. Reacting to the pattern of her thumbprint, the lock snicked back and the door swung open. Glancing in, Chaz saw an apartment like his own and

everyone else's in this area of the Dells. Then a chittering,
whining noise drew his attention to a corner of the room
behind an extruded sofa; and a strange creature came out
into the center of the apt.

It was a black-furred animal, which seemed to grow as it
emerged, until finally in the center of the room it seemed
about as large as a middling-sized dog, only much more
heavily furred. It had a long black, bushy tail, a sharp muzzle,
and eyes that glittered with what seemed to be more intelligence than a non-human creature should have. Eileen began talking to it in a strange mutter of syllables the moment
she opened the door, and when she stopped the creature
answered with its own chittering, whining, and near-barking
in a pattern that had all the cadence of a human reply.

"My pet," said Eileen, turning to Chaz. "He's a wolverine.
I call him Tillicum."

"Tillicum?" said Chaz, as jolted by the name as the identity of the species to which Eileen's pet belonged. He had
never expected to hear of, much less see, a wolverine in the
sterile areas outside of a zoo. "You call him Tillicum?"

"Yes. Why?" Eileen was staring at him penetratingly again.

"No reason," said Chaz. "It's just that the name means
'friend' in the North Pacific Coast Indian dialects; and I'd
always heard wolverines weren't all that friendly."

"You know Indian languages?" Eileen asked.

"No," said Chaz. "It's just that my head's cluttered like
an old-fashioned attic, with all sorts of information about
this and that. Like that song you were singing to the tune of
'Scarborough Fair,' back in my apt—" He broke off. "It
doesn't matter. You mean it was Tillicum you said we
needed?"

"Yes," said Eileen. She took a half-size limpet light and
some other small items from one of the drawers built into
the wall beside her, then turned. "Come on."

She turned and led the way out of the apartment. This
time it was Chaz who followed, Tillicum at his heels.

"Where are we going?" Chaz asked, as they started off down the corridor, only to stop and turn in, short of the elevator tubes, through the door leading to the emergency stairs.

"To the basement," said Eileen. She did not offer to say anything more; and Chaz followed her down the green-painted concrete steps of the stairwell that echoed to the sound of their footfalls, but not to those of Tillicum, padding noiselessly beside them.

The walk down seemed longer than Chaz had expected. He found himself trying to think when he had last traveled up or down in a building by any other way than elevator —and found he could not remember doing so since he had been a boy. Finally, however, they came to a point where the stairs ended. A heavy fire door with a bar latch faced them. Eileen leaned on it, and they went through.

They came out into a small room with the same bare, green-painted cement walls, floor, and ceiling. Another door stood in the wall to their right, with a ventilator grille to its left about six feet off the floor. Warm air poured noiselessly from the grille; and Chaz found he welcomed it. The starkness of the concrete surroundings made the room seem chilly, whether it was really so or not.

Ignoring the door, which was labeled with a sign No Admittance; Authorized Personnel Only just above the small, silver square of the door lock, Eileen stepped to the ventilator shaft and took from her pocket a rectangular brown box small enough to be hidden in her fist. She pressed this to each corner of the ventilator grille. The grille fell off, revealing the small, square black entrance to the ventilating duct.

"Why not open the door, instead, if you've got a full-band vibration key?" Chaz asked, curiously.

"Because the cycle and pitch on that door lock are changed every week by remote control from Central Computer," she answered without turning her head. "The ventilator fastenings are standard. Central doesn't worry about it because it's

too small for anyone but a child to get into; and just inside
there's a set of weighted bars too heavy for a child to lift."

"Then we're out of luck on two counts," said Chaz. "No
child, and a child would be too weak, anyhow."

"Tillicum can do it," she said, calmly.

She looked at the wolverine. Tillicum leaped the full six
feet to the duct entrance with surprising ease and vanished
inside it. Eileen turned from the opening back to Chaz.

"It'll take a few minutes," she said.

"Tillicum can get inside that way," Chaz said. "But how
about us?"

"He'll open the door for us. It's not locked from the inside," Eileen said.

"You mean," Chaz said, "he can handle ordinary door
knobs, or whatever they've got on the other side, there?"

"Yes," she said.

Chaz fell into a doubtful silence. But, a moment later, the
door swung open in front of them; and Tillicum looked up
at them, red-lined mouth half open as if in laughter.

"Come on," said Eileen.

They went in through the door, and down a corridor perhaps ten meters in length to where another door stood ajar,
held that way by a large cardboard carton that had been
pushed between it and the jamb. Chaz looked from the
carton to Tillicum, thoughtfully.

Through the second door they came to a wide, brightly lit
tunnel, down the center of which ran a broad conveyor belt
at not much more than walking speed. Where they stood was
a broad place in the tunnel, nearly filled with some sort of
automatic machinery, half of which was accepting refuse
from the condominium above, packaging it in cartons and
sending it out on the conveyor belt, while the other half
accepted cartons from those on the belt, broke them open,
and dispatched the merchandise, food, or other contents
within them upstairs to the apartments to which they were
addressed. Chaz looked at the machinery curiously. Every-

body knew about this delivery system, but he, like most, had never seen it in action.

"Good," he said to Eileen. "I ride the conveyor down to Central distributing, sneak upstairs to the Transportation Center, and I ought to be able to manage to get on a night freight train for Chicago without trouble. Once in Chicago, I can hide out until I can qualify for the Mass."

"You're that sure you can qualify?" she said.

He looked at her, a little surprised.

"I thought you believed in my working on the Mass," he answered. "As a matter of fact"—he felt in his pocket for the catalyst and found it still safely there—"I am that sure."

"All right," she said, "but you'll never make it to Chicago on your own. For one thing, there're inspectors patrolling this whole conveyor system all the time." She turned to the wolverine. "Tillicum!"

Tillicum leaped up on top of the machine that was filling empty cartons with refuse from the apartments above. Reaching down with one paw and surprising strength, he flipped a large, empty carton from the machine to the floor, then jumped back down to join Eileen and Chaz.

Eileen had already produced a small self-powered knife; and this hummed cheerfully as its vibrating blade slit the carton open vertically. She cut the top and bottom surfaces as well as the one vertical face of the carton, and then, with Tillicum humping forward to help, spread the container open like an antique wardrobe trunk.

"Yes," she said, peering into its empty interior. "Plenty of space—Tillicum!"

The wolverine, reacting as if he could read her mind, pushed the carton together again and shoved it across the floor to the conveyor belt itself. Then, taking it between both forelegs almost like a human, he jerked it upward until it tumbled on to the belt and began to be carried away.

Tillicum leaped after it and stuck his claws in the carton, setting it upright once more.

"Come on. Hurry!" said Eileen, jumping up on the belt herself. Chaz stared for a split second, then followed her. She was walking down the belt toward Tillicum and the carton. When Chaz caught up with them, she had opened the carton along her cut, and was already crawling inside.

"Come on!" she said.

Chaz frowned, but followed her. A second later, Tillicum slid in beside them and, hooking his claws in the carton, pulled the carton closed. It was a tight fit with all three of them, but the box-shape finally closed except for a crack and they were in almost total darkness. There was a faint sucking sound and a second later illumination filled the carton's interior from the limpet light Eileen had just attached to the carton side above her head.

In its white glare Chaz found himself and Eileen sitting facing each other with their knees almost touching. Tillicum was somehow curled up around and under their legs.

"But why do you want to come with me?" Chaz said.

"I told you you couldn't get out on your own," she answered. "I'm taking you someplace safe where you can wait until I can arrange to get you away."

"You're taking a chance, too," he reminded her. "Remember I've been outside. These are pretty close quarters to avoid being infected from me."

"I'm perfectly safe!" she said impatiently. "Never mind that—" She broke off. "What are you going 'hmmm,' about?"

Chaz had not realized he had made any audible sound.

"Nothing," he said. "Just, your name—never mind. What was it you were going to say?"

"I was saying, never mind that. We're as close to being safe from inspectors in this carton as we can be. Now's the chance to stop and think about covering your tracks. Do you have anybody who might come looking for you when you don't show up?"

"The office will probably call, if I don't show up there tomorrow morning," he said. "I've qualified for work in the Records Research Section at the Illinois State Center."

"I know," Eileen said. "You told me, that night in the amusement rooms. It's a pretty good job nowadays, with ten people waiting for every opening there is, just to keep from sitting on their hands doing nothing."

"It's the kind of work where that cluttered memory attic in my head comes in useful," he said. "But I don't think they'll miss me too much, even if they call a couple of times and get no answer. As you say, there's too many other people wanting to take my place."

"Good," said Eileen. "How about relatives? No relatives?"

"I didn't tell you that?" he asked, a little dryly.

"Oh, that's right. Your cousins, and your aunt," she said. "You did mention them. But I think you said you didn't get along with them."

"I don't," he said. "They took me in to raise after my father died, and my mother had been dead three years. My uncle was all right—as long as he lived—but my aunt and their kids were poisonous."

"So, they wouldn't wonder about you if you disappeared suddenly?"

"No," said Chaz. He reached into his pocket and took a firm grip on the stony surface of the catalyst. "And now that I've set your mind at ease about that, how about you doing the same for me? Don't you think it's safe now to tell me where you're taking me, and who it is you're delivering me to?"

CHAPTER FOUR

SHE DID NOT answer for a long moment, but sat staring at him in the brilliant light from the limpet. In spite of the current of air that the belt's motion pushed through the narrow gap left where the cut side and top of the carton were not completely joined together, these close quarters were becoming stuffy. Chaz thought he caught a faint, skunky odor from the wolverine at their feet.

"What are you talking about?" she said at last. "Deliver you? To who?"

"It's just a guess," he answered, still holding on to the rock. In one corner of his thoughts was the plan that if the wolverine turned on him, he would try to shove the stone down its throat—this would at least give him some kind of fighting chance. "But I don't think it's too bad a one. I mentioned this cluttered-attic mind of mine. Match that up to a talent for chain-perception, and too many things about this situation seem to hook together."

"For example?" Her face was set and her voice was brittle. When he did not answer immediately, she went on. "Who am I supposed to be delivering you to?"

"I don't know," he said. "The Citadel?"

The air hissed suddenly between her teeth on a sharp intake of breath.

"You're saying I'm connected with the criminal underworld?" she snapped. "What gives you the right—who do you think I am, anyway?"

"A Satanist?" he said, questioningly.

She made another faint breathing noise; but this time it was the sound of the breath going out of her as if knocked out by a sudden, unexpected blow. She stared at him with eyes that were abruptly round with disbelief.

"Can you read minds?" she said, faintly.

He shook his head.

"No," he said, "I don't pretend to any paranormal talents —except for chain-perception. You ought to know there's no such thing as a true telepath, anyway."

"There's other ways to know things," she said, still a little obscurely. "What makes you say I'm a Satanist?"

"A lot of little things," he said. "Your name, for one."

"My name?"

"Mortvain," he said. "If you were a French-speaking knight in the Middle Ages, with that as a motto under the heraldic achievement on your shield, I'd be pretty sure you were defying death."

"Death?" She shook her head. "Me? I defy death?"

"Don't you?" he answered. "At least twice you've told me that you're not afraid of my infecting you with rot, in spite of the fact you know I've been exposed; and we're jammed in here so close now that you could hardly help getting spores from my breath if I've already been infected, myself."

"I just meant . . . I don't believe you could have been infected," she said. "A short time outside like that."

"How do you know how long I was outside?"

"Well, it couldn't have been long. Anyway, what's that got to do with my name?"

"I think you already know," he said. "Mortvain. Mortvain, from the Old French '*Mort*,' meaning 'death' and '*en vein*'—meaning 'without success,' or perhaps 'in a blasphemous manner.' Freely translated, your name could mean 'I defy death' or 'I blaspheme against death.'"

"That's nonsense," she said.

"You're saying, then, that you don't hold with Satanist beliefs?" he said, watching her closely.

"I'm not—there's no reason why I should," she said. "Naturally, I'm not against someone else's pattern of ethos-involvement, any more than anyone else is. But that doesn't mean I've got anything to do with Satanists. Only—I'm not on trial. I don't have to assure you of anything."

"Of course not," Chaz said. "But it's a fact there are people among the Satanists who consider themselves witches. And these witches recite spells, pray rather than meditate, have animals they consider familiars, and believe that they can defy death itself as long as they are in love with a particular concept of evil. Also, as a matter of fact, they actually are supposed to be involved with organized crime."

"No," she said, her eyes half closed as if he was questioning her under duress.

"No what?" he asked. "No, you're not involved with organized crime? Or no, you're not a witch?"

Her eyes opened at that. She even smiled faintly.

"Have you stopped beating your wife?" she murmured. "What kind of a choice are you giving me?"

Her smile made him smile back in spite of himself. But he stuck to the point.

"All right," he said. "I put the question badly. Bluntly—are you someone who thinks she's a witch?"

"And if I was?" she said. "What difference would it make? I'm helping you anyway."

"Or delivering me to someone."

"No!" she said suddenly and violently. "I'd never turn you

over, to anyone. I'm no criminal—and no Satanist!" The
violence leaked out of her unexpectedly; and she looked at
him again squarely. "But, all right. You're not wrong about
one thing. I am a witch. Only it's pretty plain you don't know
anything about what that means."

"I thought I'd just shown you I knew quite a bit," Chaz
said.

"And they say prejudice is dead!" Her voice was bitter.
"Haven't you ever learned that witches always were people
with paranormal talents, who had no place else to go in the
past, but into devil-worshiping communities? You'd be
pretty upset if I called *you* a Satanist, just because you believe you've got a talent for Heisenbergian chain-perception."

Chaz had to admit to himself that this was true.

"You turned up pretty conveniently right after the wreck
and before the woman came, though," he said.

"I've got paranormal talents, too, of course!" she flared.
"Why do you think I bother myself about you? Because
we're both different. We're both on the outside, shut away
from ordinary people, looking in. That's why it matters to me
what happens to you!"

"I don't consider myself on the outside looking in," he
said, obscurely angry.

"Oh, no?" Her voice was scornful. She went on as if reciting from a dossier. "Charles Roumi Sant. Always in trouble
in primary and secondary schools. Anti-Neopuritanist. Candidate for degrees in nearly a dozen fields before he managed
to graduate in System Patterns."

"You know a lot about me," he said, grimly.

"I took the trouble to find out, after that evening down
in the party rooms," she said. "The trouble with you,
Charles Roumi Sant, is that you think your own talents are
real, but mine have to be some kind of fake, or part of some
con game."

"No—" Chaz began, and then his conscience tripped him
up before he got any farther. Once more he had to admit
that she was right.

"This is the twenty-first century," he said, instead. "Everybody knows there's no such thing as the supernatural, or supernatural powers."

"Paranormal, I said. Not supernatural!" she retorted. "Just like you, and yours. There's that prejudice I was talking about. Because someone like me uses the old word 'witch' you think she's a charlatan. Well, I'm not. I was the one who saved you from that train wreck, whether you know it, or not!"

Her words seemed to trigger off something like a soundless explosion in his head.

"No, you didn't!" he said. "I saved myself. I did any saving that was done!"

The wolverine snarled lightly under his knees; but the warning was not needed. As soon as the words were out of his mouth, he had felt the backwash of his own sudden fury and been jarred by it. But not jarred to the point of taking back what he had just said.

"All right," he went on in a more level voice. "I'm not going to fly off the handle. But don't fool yourself. I got myself out of that train wreck situation by using chain-perception; and I know how I did it, every step of the way. I used—" He broke off, on the point of talking about the catalyst. "Never mind. You were going to tell me what witches were really like. How did someone like you end up as one?"

"I didn't end up!" she said. "I was born one. Just as you were born the way *you* are. My mother and grandmother were witches; and thought of themselves as witches. Only, by the time I came along, psychology knew enough about the phenomenon so that I could separate the superstitions about us from the reality. Of course, I knew all about the superstitions. I heard enough about them from the older people. In fact, when I was a little girl, I believed them, too; until I learned better in school and university."

"All right," Chaz said again. Emotion had been strong in her voice; and that had gotten through to him more deeply than the actual words she had been saying. "Most of the old ideas about witches are superstition. What's real, then?"

"The basis," she said. "We actually can do things. But we have to be emotionally convinced we can do them before our paranormal abilities will work. In fact, that's a sort of basic law for all people with such abilities. Stop and think for a minute. Do you think you could use this chain-perception of yours if you suddenly started doubting you could?"

"Hmm. No," said Chaz, suddenly reminded of what Waka had said about most candidates for work on the Pritcher Mass being self-convinced about their abilities.

"Of course not," Eileen went on. "It's like anything above the normal. The creative frenzy of an artist. The way an athlete surpasses himself under pressure. It takes a complete, wholehearted commitment to the idea that you can do what you want to do. . . ."

She went on talking; but Chaz's attention slipped slightly from what she was saying. He had just become aware that the vibration of the belt beneath them had gradually increased, and the air coming through the crack in the carton was now a breeze moving fast enough to cause a whistle. Holding up a hand to interrupt Eileen, he leaned over to put his eye to the crack and look outside.

What he saw were concrete walls now flickering past rapidly. The belt had increased its speed several times over. Just how fast they were going now, he had no way to estimate; but it was certainly enough that any attempt to get off the belt on to the narrow service walkway running along one of its sides would mean serious injury or even death. He brought his head back and looked at Eileen in the glare of the limpet light.

"Where are we?" he asked.

"Getting close to Central Distributing," she said. "Almost to the place where we get off."

"Get off?"

"You'll see," she said. He thought, but could not be sure, that he caught the gleam of a secret satisfaction in her eyes at seeing him sweat out the descent from the belt without knowing how it was to be done. He clamped his own jaws shut; and for the next few minutes, neither of them said anything.

Abruptly, she and Tillicum moved together, spreading the carton wide open, so that they sat exposed on the belt. Eileen rose from a sitting position into a crouch.

"Get ready," she told him. "There'll be an overflow belt swinging in alongside this one in a few seconds. When it's parallel, get ready to jump."

"At this speed?" Chaz said. But she did not answer. He got into a crouching position himself; and a moment or two later saw a dark spot on the right side of the tunnel up ahead, which grew rapidly to reveal itself as the mouth of a connecting tunnel. A belt ran through this, too, curving in as Eileen had said to parallel the one they were on. But it was several feet below the surface of their present carrier.

"Ready . . ." said Eileen. They flashed toward the point where the two belts ran side by side. *"Now!"*

Chaz jumped, a little behind Eileen. Behind him, out of the corner of his eye, he could see Tillicum flying through the air as gracefully as a cat. Then they hit.

He had braced himself against the landing. But it was like coming down on a barely filled water bed. There was none of the impact Chaz had expected; and no tendency whatever for the momentum they carried from the former belt to send them sliding or rolling.

It was then he realized that this second belt also was moving. Naturally, he thought, disgusted at his own lack of imagination, the speeds of the two belts had been matched—or almost—at the point where they changed over. They could possibly even have stood up to make the transfer—

No, on second thought, standing up might not have been so wise. Because, Chaz realized, even as he was thinking this, the second belt was decelerating sharply. It had curved away from the main belt into a further tunnel; and now he saw the end of that tunnel, expanded into a fair-sized room half filled with sorting tables leading to smaller belts disappearing off into further tunnel ports.

"This is a secondary sorting center—for when the main belt gets overloaded," Eileen was saying; and then they reached the end of the belt where it turned down abruptly to disappear into a slot in the floor. It tumbled them gently on to the floor at a good deal less than slow walking speed.

"A variable-speed belt," said Chaz, marveling, picking himself up. "How do they do that?"

He broke off, having glanced back along the belt and seen how they did that. Every five meters or so they had been passed on from one belt to another, each traveling at a slightly slower speed.

"However," Eileen was saying, now back on her feet also, "in the fall, like this, it never gets overloaded. After holidays, when a lot of people come back to their apartments at once, is the only time you can be sure to find it working. So it's pretty safe here right now."

"I'm supposed to hole up here?" Chaz asked, looking around him.

"No," said Eileen. "Come along."

She led the way, Tillicum beside her, past the sorting tables toward two doors, one marked *Men* and one *Women*. She beckoned Chaz to follow and led him through the door marked *Women*. The first room was a carpeted lounge. Within, along one wall was a long mirror, coming to within two feet of the floor and an equal distance from the three-meter-high ceiling. Eileen touched the two bottom corners of the mirror lightly with the tip of her index finger, stood back, and clapped her hands, once. The mirror pivoted about its midpoint, one end retreating into the wall, the other swinging out into the lounge to reveal a hidden room, about the size of the lounge. Eileen stepped over the low ledge of wall into this room. Tillicum followed with an easy leap, and Chaz stepped over after the wolverine.

"Stand clear," said Eileen. Chaz moved aside and she touched the mirror. It swung back into place, shutting them in without visible exits.

Chaz looked around. There was a dais at one end of the room, with an elaborate, high-backed chair of what looked like carved wood upon it. Folding chairs were scattered about the gray concrete floor, apart from the dais.

"I thought you said you weren't a Satanist," he said to Eileen. "Isn't this one of their secret temples?"

"No, it isn't," she said. "As a matter of fact, it's a witches' hole. But I don't expect you to know the difference."

His conscience bit him—hard.

"I'm sorry," he said. "I really do appreciate what you're trying to do for me. I'm not trying to needle you. It just comes out that way, sometimes."

"I've noticed that," she retorted, then softened in turn. "All right. Never mind. We might as well sit down, now. We have to wait for someone."

"Who?" he said. "Or should I ask?"

"Of course you should ask," she said. "It's someone we call the Gray Man."

"A warlock?"

"Not a warlock. A male witch!" she said. "A warlock's— well, never mind. Actually, the old distinctions don't matter. He's just another one of us with paranormal talents; but in his case, he stands in a position which links the witch group to the non-witch group."

Chaz frowned.

"I don't follow you," he said.

"All right, then," Eileen answered. "He's our link with the criminal underworld, the Citadel—I know, I told you we didn't have anything to do with the Citadel!" she added swiftly. "We don't, we full witches. But the connection has always been there, and sometimes it's useful for us. Like now. The Citadel can hide you until you can qualify for the Pritcher Mass. I can't."

"What if this Gray Man doesn't go along with you?" Chaz asked, feeling for the rock in his pocket instinctively.

"He will." Her eyes flashed. "He gives away half his strength by making himself a servant of non-witches. Any one of us full witches is stronger than he is. I can make him do anything I want."

"*Anything?*" said a voice that seemed to echo strangely about them, from no particular individual source. Chaz glanced in several directions before realizing that the ornate chair on the dais was now occupied. The slim, wide-shouldered figure sitting in it was dressed in a tight-fitting gray jumpsuit; but it also wore gray gloves and shoes, and its head and neck were completely covered by an elastic gray mask that showed a bald, eyelashless, expressionless face of the sort that might be found on an old-fashioned department store dummy. The figure looked small; but the size of the chair might have contributed to that. In addition, Chaz found, there seemed to be some distortion in the air about the gray figure, so that it was hard to keep it in focus for more than a few seconds without blinking.

"Anything I really want and need!" Eileen was answering, fiercely. "Are you challenging me?"

"Sister—dear sister—" said the voice that seemed to come from all around them as the lips of the mask stayed motionless, "let's not argue. Of course I'm happy to do what any one of you want. What is it this time?"

"I want this man here kept safe from the law until he can qualify for work on the Pritcher Mass. He'll need to stay in the Chicago area."

"Just that? Is that all, sister?" The tone of the omnidirectional voice was ironic.

"That'll do for now." Her voice was hard.

"It could be done. Of course," said the Gray Man. "I can do anything, let alone that. But should I? You've never been kind to me like some of the others, sister."

"You know I don't have to be!" Eileen snapped. "I'm not

one of the old ones who thinks she needs you. There's no covenant between us. So don't try to play one of your little games with me. You get paid by the Citadel for what we do for you when we feel like it. But you do what we say because you've got no choice."

"No choice? How sad."

"Stop wasting time!" said Eileen. "I've got to get back to my apartment. Have you got some place in mind you can keep Mr. Sant, here, until he passes his Pritcher Mass test?"

"Oh yes," said the Gray Man. "I've got a lovely place. It's in a big building, but he won't mind that. It's very quiet and very dark, but he won't mind that. In fact, after a while he won't mind anything."

Eileen stared at him for a long second.

"Have you gone completely insane?" she asked finally, in a low, cold voice. "Or are you actually challenging me?"

"Challenging you? Oh no, sister," said the Gray Man, spreading his hands. "I've just got no choice. It's the Citadel that wants Mr. Sant out of the way; and he wasn't cooperative enough to stay nicely outside where the train wreck put him. Of course, his coming back in put him on the wrong side of the law and that makes it easier for us."

"*Us?* You class yourself all the way with criminals, now?" said Eileen. "Not that it matters. What's the Citadel got to do with him?"

"That they don't tell me, sister. They only told me to bring him to them—just as soon as you brought him to me. And so I must, now."

"Must? I've had enough of this!" Eileen said. "It's time you remembered who you're talking to. Tillicum—"

The wolverine moved—and froze again, as Eileen suddenly flung out her hand to stop him. A hand laser had appeared in one of the gray-gloved hands of the figure on the dais. Holding the weapon, the Gray Man threw back his head; and his laughter beat upon them from all sides.

"Sister! Dear sister!" he said. "Do you think I'd risk anything like this unless I knew you were powerless? Stop and think. Has anything worked for you lately? Has even the smallest work of the Great Art succeeded for you?"

"What are you talking about?" said Eileen.

"You know. You know!" the Gray Man crowed like a delighted baby. "You're in *love*, sister dear. You've done what no witch can ever do, and get away with. You fell in love and so you've lost your power!"

"I told you I wasn't one of the old ones!" said Eileen, furiously. "I know what my powers are—natural paranormal talents. I can't lose them by falling in love, any more than I can lose an arm or a leg."

"Of course you can't! Oh, of course!" crowed the Gray Man. "You can't lose them—but you can't use them. Because you believed the old tales when you were a child; and the primitive part of your mind can't get rid of that belief, can it? Of course love didn't take away your talents, sister dear. But it gave you a psychological block that keeps you from using them. Doesn't it—"

Eileen stepped back a step and threw up her hands, crossing the first two fingers of the left hand over the first two fingers of the right, before her face, so that she looked through the square these fingers made, at the Gray Man. She spoke swiftly:

"*Light curses dark, and both curse gray.*
"*A tree, a rock, a shrieking jay,*
"*Will hear you moan at break of day.*
"*Pater sonris maleorum . . .*"

"No use! No use!" shouted the Gray Man, rolling around in his seat in a fit of laughter. "Words, that's all you've got left. Words! Now *I'll* take the man."

He pointed a forefinger of his free hand at Chaz; and without warning sound and sight were cut off. Chaz found himself elsewhere.

CHAPTER FIVE

HIS FIRST thought was that the transfer had been immediate. But then the feeling followed that perhaps unconsciousness and some time had intervened between the last thing he remembered and this.

This was nothingness. A dark, solid and endless, encompassed him. He seemed either fixed in it like the corpse of a fly in amber, or afloat in its infinite regions. He could feel nothing on his skin, not even warmth or coolness. He could not even be sure he breathed.

About him there was absolute silence—or was there? He became aware then of a slow, very slow, sound repeated regularly. He was baffled for a moment, and then he recognized it as the beating of his own heart. For the first time a suspicion woke in his mind. He made a deliberate effort to turn his head to the right, then to the left. There was no way for him to tell that his head had actually moved; but, as he made the effort, he heard a grating sound that seemed to come from behind him. He knew then what his situation was, even if his knowing was little help.

The grating sound was the noise of his neck vertebrae in movement. He must be hearing it by sound conduction through the bones of his spine and skull. So slight a sound could only be audible if he was in a total isolation chamber of some sort, possibly afloat in some liquid medium, restrained so that he could not feel the restraints; but held securely enough so that he could not free himself. The isolation chamber was an ancient sort of device, dating back into the twentieth century, but not therefore a harmless one. Enough hours in this situation with all sensory input cut off and he could lose his memory. Or his mind could become a blank page on which his captors could impress any belief they wanted.

He strained to reach out with both arms and legs, to touch something—anything. But he felt nothing. He could not even tell for sure if his arms and legs had obeyed him, except by the faint sound of creaking muscles that reached his ears. He stopped trying to touch his surroundings and simply lay there. It was easiest just to lie still . . .

He caught himself drifting off into sleep; and struggled back to awareness on the body adrenalin released by his own alarm. He did not dare sleep. Somehow he had to stay awake and find some way of giving dimension to his situation. If he only had a means of simply measuring time, he could use that as a mental anchor point. He thought suddenly of his heartbeats and began to count them. One . . . two . . . three . . . His normal pulse, he knew, was around sixty-five beats per minute in a resting state. Say that in this situation it was even slower, perhaps sixty a minute only. Sixty . . . sixty-one . . .

It was no use. He began to get the impression that he was no longer hanging motionless; but sliding off down some vast, lightless slope that went on to infinity. Faster he slid, and faster. He was rocketing through the darkness now, without feeling a thing, headed out toward the very end of the universe. . . .

He was far off in space, sliding beyond all galaxies at some immeasurable multiple of the speed of light, and accelerating still. He was being carried along by a current, a swift river of nothingness cutting through the stationary nothingness that was the rest of the infinite. He was alone . . . no, he was not completely alone. Two bright spots were barely visible, far off on either side of the invisible rushing river that carried him forward so swiftly. The spots grew into shapes and came closer, shining with their own light in the darkness, until they paced him on either side of the river, traveling under their own power, but keeping level with him. They were two he had seen before. On his left was one of the massive Snails he had dreamed about when he had been unconscious in his apartment, the other was the insectile, mantis-like alien to whom he had talked in the same dream.

"Help me," he said to the Mantis, now.

"Sorry," said the Mantis. "Ethics doesn't obligate us that far."

He looked over at the Snail.

"Help me!" he said to the Snail. But the Snail neither answered nor showed any reaction, merely kept moving level with him.

"There's no point talking to him," said the Mantis. "When you talk to me, you talk to him, anyway. And when I talk to you, I tell you what he thinks as well."

"Why won't one of you help me?" Chaz said, desperately. "All you have to do is pull me out of this river. Just pull me to the side a little and I can stop."

"True," said the Mantis. "But among other ethical laws, the one of hands-off forbids us to do that. You have to get a member of the union that unplugged you to plug you back in again. It's a breach of our own contract if we do it."

The two of them began to angle off from him, dwindling into the blackness.

"Wait!" Chaz called desperately. "What union is it that I have to get to plug me in again? Tell me the name of the union!"

"There isn't any!" floated back the tiny voice of the now-distant Mantis. "It hasn't been organized yet."

They disappeared, like pinpoints of light gone out. Left alone, accelerating on the river of darkness, Chaz felt his consciousness dwindling as the Snail and Mantis had dwindled, shrinking down to a candle point, to a spark, almost ready to go out.

If only he had his catalyst, he thought. If he could apply chain-perception to this situation maybe he could find a way out, even from this.

If he had some alternatives to choose between . . . wait. He could still choose to turn his head, or not to turn his head. He could choose to move his arms or legs or not to move them. He could choose to move his right arm or his left. . . .

That was no use, either. He needed the catalyst, if only for a few seconds. He tried to imagine the stony feel of it in his hand. Imagine, he told himself. Imagine it.

He concentrated. He could almost feel the rock fitting into his grip. It was about the size of a small orange, he remembered. Its surface was rough. One small lump on its surface nestled almost comfortably between the bases of his index and second finger when his hand was closed around the rock. The surface the little finger had rested on was almost planar. A graininess irritated the heel of his hand as he tightened his grip on it. It was just this heavy. . . .

He could *feel* it.

He could feel it there in his right hand now, as real as it had ever felt in his grasp.

—And he was no longer sliding down the endless river in darkness. He was back, afloat or whatever once more in the isolation chamber, as he had been when he first awoke.

The warm flood of a tremendous feeling of triumph washed through him. He had his catalyst. He could do anything now. He held it. He could feel it. Why shouldn't he be able to see it as well?

He lifted his right hand toward his face. There was no way of telling whether he actually held it before his eyes or not; but he felt more strongly every second that he did. It was there. If it was there, he could see it.

He stared into the darkness.

Naturally, he told himself, he would not just suddenly see it, all at once. But perhaps gradually. . . . He stared into blackness and thought he saw a faint pinprick of light, such as the Snail and the Mantis had made when they had first appeared, and just before disappearing. He concentrated on it, willing it to come nearer as they had come nearer. Slowly, painfully, it grew in brightness and size. It came closer. . . .

It came to him. He held the catalyst before his face and saw it plainly, every slant and angle and color in it. As he stared at it, it blurred and changed form.

He looked down a maze of alternate choices in the pattern he had seen before—like the edges of cards in a deck slightly spread out. Plainly, he read the message in them. Of course! Whoever had put him in this had not intended to leave him here forever; only until his sanity was sufficiently softened or dissolved. Someone would be coming to take him out, eventually. Until that time, he and the catalyst would find his mind some sanity-saving work to do. . . . Of course. He almost chuckled to himself. In the infinity of darkness they could even create and build themselves a Pritcher Mass of their own right here on Earth, as it had been in his dream.

They went to work . . . and a Pritcher Mass began to take form. . . .

—Like an explosion, light blared suddenly against Chaz's closed eyelids, and the nearly completed Pritcher Mass was swept away, back into a corner of his mind. He lay limply with eyes still closed, and felt hands moving about him, heard the splash of liquid and the sound of buckles being unbuckled. There were faint pulls on his arms and legs.

"Right," a man's voice said distantly. "Lift, now."

Chaz felt himself raised by hands gripping his shoulders and legs, moved through a small arc of distance and laid on a surface which, after the isolation chamber and its lack of physical sensation, seemed shockingly hard. He kept his eyes closed. Hands moved about him, stripping some kind of helmet off his head and pulling off him tight-fitting, elastic clothing.

With the clothing off, warm air wrapped his whole body. After the silence of the chamber, every sound that was made seemed to roar in his ears. He heard the two that were working on him breathing like elephants. He heard the scrape of their feet on the floor as they turned and walked away from him, to begin sloshing and clanking noises back where he had been.

He opened his eyes and turned his head.

He lay on a white-sheeted bed in what appeared to be a hospital room with a blue curtain drawn across its transparent front wall. Two men, both in white coats, were standing with their backs to him, working on a black, rectangular box the size of two coffins placed one on top of the other. For a second the light dazzled Chaz's eyes; and then his vision settled down.

He swung his legs over the side of the bed, stood up, and took one step toward the two men. They did not hear him coming.

He hit one at the back base of the skull with what Chaz thought was the catalyst rock—until he realized that his fist had been empty. Even without the rock, it was a crushing blow with a sudden, almost berserk, fury in Chaz powering it. The man he had hit went to his knees and fell over sideways. The other man began to turn with an astonished look on his face; and Chaz leaped on him, knocking him to the floor, beating away at him as he fell with fists and knees, in a silent frenzy of attack.

It was a few seconds before Chaz realized that the second

man was not moving either and he could make himself stop.
When he did stop and scrambled to his feet his fury ebbed,
leaving him feeling sick and helpless. His stomach heaved,
but there was nothing in it to come up. He clung gratefully
to the side of the isolation chamber to keep from falling, as
his trembling legs threatened to give way.

The nausea and the trembling passed. The two on the floor
still had not stirred. He could not bring himself to look at
either man's face. Luckily, the first one he had attacked lay
face down. Without turning him over, Chaz managed to strip
off the man's clothes, including the white coat, and put them
on his own naked body. He turned to the curtain, pulled it
aside, and located the door of the hospital room.

Opening the door a crack, he peered out.

What he saw was an ordinary, circular hospital ward with
two nurses inside the round desk area that occupied the
ward's center point. Both of them had their heads bent over
some paper work at the moment. Holding his breath, Chaz
opened the door a little further, stepped through, closed it
behind him, and walked casually toward the entrance to
the ward, a quarter of the way around the circle of rooms.

Neither of the two nurses looked up. A second later he was
in a wide corridor, busy with hospital personnel and visitors
alike. Three minutes later he was alone in a four-seater P.R.T.
car leaving the basement of the hospital for the Central Terminal, courtesy of the credit card in a pocket of the man
whose clothes he had taken.

As the car hurtled through the tunnelways, Chaz glanced
over the stations listed on the car's directory and saw that he
was in the Chicago area, evidently up around Evanston. Chicago had been too big to seal as a single sterile unit; and to
this day it was a number of connected domes and under-
ground areas. It was this ramshackle character of the big city
that had given him hope that he could manage to evade capture in it long enough to see Waka again and pass the test for

work on the Pritcher Mass. Now, with someone else's credit card, his chances were even better.

Of course, the man from whom he had taken the clothes and the card could report the card stolen—although, if he was really a member of the Citadel, he might not want to tell the police how he had lost it. But even if the card was reported lost, Chicago was so large that by the time the Central Computer got police sent to the last place he had used it, he could be miles away. In twenty-four hours, of course, all automated units of the Chicago area could be programmed to refuse that particular card when it was submitted to a computer outlet for credit or purchase. But in twenty-four hours he ought to be able to see Waka, pass the test, and get officially accepted for work on the Mass. Once he was accepted, all Earth's police could do would be to keep him under room arrest until time for him to ship out to the Mass.

Things were looking up. Chaz relaxed and even grinned a little to himself, remembering the astonished look on the face of the first man he had jumped, back in the hospital room. Plainly, the last thing they had expected was that their sensorily-deprived patient would have as much energy left in him as Chaz had shown.

But then he sobered. He might be free now, but in addition to the police, the Citadel would be after him—and why should they have been interested in him in the first place? He had never had anything to do with the criminal element of the sterile world. He did not even know much, if anything, about it beyond what he, like everyone else, heard on the news, or read in the magfax.

He tried to marshal what meager knowledge he had, so that he could get some idea of what he might be up against. But there was little even in the attic section of his mind to go on. In a cashless society, of course, the criminal element operated by markedly different tactics than they had in the bad old days when credit was expressed in pieces of paper you carried about and traded with other people. Now, credit

was hardly more than a convenience. What really paid off
was power: power to control the credit ratings and the class
of the cards that were computer-issued to you or your asso-
ciates; power to compel people to provide goods or services
that could not ordinarily be bought, or that were out-and-
out illegal; power to tap the wide, unsterile areas for things
that might not be available within the limited space of the
sterile ones.

Of course, it was that last reported power of the Citadel
that led to the strong belief that it, unlike any other element
of society, had contacts outside the sterile areas. Though
who these contacts could be with, since anyone who stayed
outside could hardly last more than a month or two before
dying of Job's-berry rot, was a question. What could you offer
a dying person to buy his or her services? Comforts? Drugs?
Luxuries?

Not being a Neopuritan, Chaz paid no attention to the
legend that there were rare people outside who had survived
the rot. That was nonsense. The rot was not a chemical or
viral thing that sickened the body. Its effect was purely mechanical. The spores in the air sooner or later found their
way into the lungs of anyone unshielded. There they sprouted
and grew, until eventually the lungs were too choked to func-
tion. Immunity did not enter into the situation; any more
than the Neopuritanic belief that the rot, and its parent, the
Job's-berry, were a judgment upon man for his sins in polluting and despoiling the world.

No, there was no need to get scriptural about it. Planet-
wide pollution had led to plant mutations; and plant mutations had led to the Job's-berry. The Job's-berry would lead
to the end of the human race. There was nothing the remnant
of humanity existing in the shielded, sterile areas could do
now to exterminate the plant and clean the world's air. All
they could hope for was to fight a losing battle; long enough
for the Pritcher Mass workers to find another habitable

world, to which a select handful of the race could emigrate, so that the race itself could survive and make a fresh start.

Chaz reined in his thoughts with a jerk. The little P.R.T. car was almost to the Central Terminal destination he had punched at random when he got into the vehicle. He consulted the directory again and repunched for the location of Waka's office. The directory clicked and showed the change in its destination window.

He sat back, his mind now off on another topic. What had happened to Eileen? She had seemed perfectly sure of herself up to the point where she had tried to use her witchcraft to discipline the Gray Man; and the Gray Man had laughed at her. What happened to a witch who lost her abilities? Chaz ransacked his mental attic without turning up any information on that point. For the first time he considered the possibility that she might be in the hands of the Citadel, just as he had been; and a cold hand seemed to take a firm grip on his stomach.

Of course, she had been helping him; and since it was this that had gotten her into trouble, if she was in trouble, it was not surprising to find himself concerned about her. On the other hand, it was surprising that, with the little time they had been together, she should have gotten so firmly caught in the gears of his emotions. He had always thought of himself as a loner with a cynical view of his fellow men and women; the last man in the world likely to find himself feeling undue affection for anyone on short notice. Unless . . . they had somehow gotten to know each other unusually well that night of the condominium party. He wished he could remember more clearly what had gone on. In fact, once he had a moment, he should sit down and dig those memories out. Nothing in the mental attic could hide from him if he went after it determinedly enough.

The P.R.T. car slid on through tunnels and came to dockage finally in the basement of the building in which Waka had his office, and possibly his living quarters as well. Chaz got out, more awkwardly and creakily than he had expected. His sudden explosion of activity after lying in that coffin-like isolation chamber for an unguessable number of hours had apparently strained muscles. He felt as stiff as a football player the day after a game.

He walked up and down, swinging his arms in the privacy of the momentarily empty P.R.T. dock. The exercise loosened him up and got his blood flowing again. He turned toward the elevator tubes and then remembered that he was still wearing the white hospital jacket. He took it off and stuffed it into a recycle-tube slot at one end of the dock. This left him dressed in slacks and a short-sleeved white shirt. Not exactly a jumpsuit—but not odd enough either to attract undue attention.

He took the tube up to Waka's office but found the door to it locked. He walked down the corridor of the floor he was on until he came to a rank of phones. Sticking his credit card into the slot of the first one he came to, he punched for Central Locating and asked it to see if Mr. Alexander Waka could be found and communicated with.

There was a small wait while CL worked. Then a chime sounded from the phone grille and the screen lit up with a miniature image of Waka's head and bare shoulders.

"I'm at home," said Waka. "Is this an emergency? Oh— Mr. Sant."

"It's an emergency," Chaz said. "I need to be tested immediately."

"Immediately?" Waka looked doubtful. "I don't think I can do that."

"Isn't it your duty to take a Pritcher Mass candidate at any hour?" Chaz said. "Sorry, Mr. Waka. But it *is* an emergency. Emergency enough so that I'm ready to complain to the authorities, if I have to, to get a test right away. A complaint like that could cost an examiner his license."

Waka smiled. A small, hard smile.

"You might be interested to know, Mr. Sant," he said,

"I've had a call from Police Central about you. Are you sure you're ready to contact the authorities yourself, just to complain about me?"

Chaz looked back at him for a second.

"So much for that commitment to the Pritcher Mass you were telling me about last time I saw you," he said.

Waka stayed where he was, frowning.

"All right," he answered, abruptly. "Apartment 4646B, the same tower you're in. Come on up."

He cut contact and the screen went blank.

Chaz punched off the phone at his end. For a second he leaned against the phone stand in relief. It was all over but the test now; and the test should be no problem. It was true he no longer had the catalyst; but in the isolation chamber imagining that he held it worked just as well.

Still leaning against the phone, he half closed his eyes and made an effort to feel the rock once more in his hand. It was about the size of an orange. A little roughness on it fitted almost comfortably between his first two fingers. . . .

He stood there, making the effort to imagine it. Evidently, however, conceiving something like this was much easier inside an isolation chamber than outside one. Slowly it grew on him that now, just standing here as he was, he did not seem to be able to convince himself that the catalyst was really with him.

CHAPTER SIX

HE STAYED where he was for a good ten minutes, working with his imagination in an attempt to visualize the catalyst in the real sense in which he had visualized it while he had been in the isolation chamber. But he could not convince himself that he was succeeding—and, worse, he could not feel the confidence he had felt in the isolation chamber, or earlier at the train wreck, when the catalyst had been physically in his hand.

Still, he kept trying. He only gave up after he had been stared at several times by people going and coming from offices along the corridor and he began to fear that he was becoming conspicuous.

Waka would not wait forever. Chaz headed toward the elevator tubes, still working to make his imagination build the feel of a rock in his hand, the confidence of a catalyst in his mind.

Chaz was on the twelfth level of the building he was in. It

was normal for offices to be on the lower levels, apartments on the upper. Anything over thirty stories was somewhat unusual, but Chicago went back to the days of tall buildings. He stepped aboard an up-floating disk and let it carry him skyward.

At the forty-sixth level he got off and went down a much narrower hallway than the one he had left below until he came to a doorway of imitation walnut, with the figures 4646B glowing on it. He knocked, and the door opened immediately—as if Waka had been standing waiting behind it.

The examiner grunted, seeing Chaz; and then, sticking his head out into the corridor, looked up and down swiftly. Dressed now in a blue sleeping robe, he was not the Waka whom Chaz was used to seeing during office hours. This man was harder of manner, and at the same time furtive. He pulled his head back in, beckoned Chaz curtly inside the apartment, and closed the door.

Inside, the apartment was more luxurious than any Chaz had seen since his childhood. There was a kitchenette at one end of the room he entered and, at the room's other end, was an open door which gave a glimpse of an unusual extra chamber, apparently furnished for nothing but sleeping.

"What took you so long?" Waka demanded. His phone chimed. "Wait here."

He turned and went into the sleeping room, closing the door behind him. Chaz could hear him answering the phone from in there. The murmur of his voice was audible, but it was not possible to make out the words.

Chaz was left standing in the middle of the main room of the luxury apartment. It was the sort of place that would have made a fine large home for a couple with a pre-school child or two. For some reason, Eileen returned to his thoughts with a poignancy he could hardly bear. She had deserved better than what he had brought her. Somewhere, there could be no doubt about it, she was in trouble—whether in the hands of the Citadel or the police.

The worst part was there was nothing he could do to help her. At least—nothing he could do unless he could pass the Pritcher Mass test now and end his own need to keep running. It all depended on his passing that test. Once more he made the effort to imagine the feel of the catalyst in his fist.

It would not come. Anger twisted itself up like a tight, hard knot within him. There was no good reason he should not be able to evoke the catalyst. For that matter, he ought to be able to pass the test even without it. Either he had the talent to pass, or he did not; and he knew he had it. Letting anything get in the way was as ridiculous as Eileen letting some childish superstition get in the way of her talents when she had tried to control the Gray Man. What was it the Gray Man had accused her of having—a psychological block? That was nothing more than his own trouble with the catalyst in different form. The catalyst was a psychological prop—an emotional prop, for that matter—in his case.

The thought of the catalyst as nothing more than a prop brought a sense of relief to him. It was as if, somewhere inside him, a barrier had gone down. But before he had time to examine the feeling of relief, Waka came back.

"That was Communications Central, running what they said was a routine spot check," Waka said. "When you called here, were you using somebody else's credit card?"

"That's right," said Chaz.

"Get rid of it, then; before they catch you with it on you, will you?" Waka was not obviously sweating, but he passed a hand across his forehead as if to wipe away perspiration. "Do you realize records will show that particular card made a call to my number? If they connect the card with you, it'll be known you called me."

"What difference would that make?" Chaz asked, looking at the examiner closely. "It's natural I'd make one last try to get accepted for the Mass. And, once accepted, the authorities can't do anything to me—or you."

"You don't understand," said Waka, shortly. He turned

away to sit down at a small table—a real table, not one extruded from floor or wall. He opened a drawer and took out
a pair of achromatic goggles and a tube of mixed colors. "Sit
down. Just get rid of it, I tell you."

Chaz seated himself.

"Who are you worried about, except the authorities?" he
asked. He looked thoughtfully at Waka. "You don't happen to have anything to do with the Citadel yourself?"

"Put on the glasses," said Waka, shoving them across the
table top. "What color do you want to try to separate from
the rest?"

"Wait a minute." Chaz let the glasses lie. "The only people you could be worried about would have to be from the
Citadel. But if you belong to them, why are you giving me
this test? From what I've seen so far, for some reason the
last place the Citadel wants me is on the Mass. How is it
you're giving me a chance to go there?"

"Because I'm a goddamn fool!" burst out Waka. "Stop
asking questions! Put on the glasses."

Chaz picked them up, but he did not immediately put
them on.

"Tell me something else, first," he said. "Just one more
thing; and then I'll put them on and we can get into the test.
Did you ever know anybody you thought ought to qualify for
work on the Mass, but who didn't seem to be able to pass
the test because of some psychological block?"

"Yes, yes—of course! I told you they were always self-
convinced if they did it! Now, if you don't start taking this
test right away, I'm not going to give it to you. Choose a
color."

"Right," said Chaz.

He spoke absent-mindedly. A strange thing was happening
inside him. It was as if his inner world of personal knowledge
was being turned upside down so that what had been west
was now east and north had become south. If Waka was telling the truth, and his own inner feelings were correct, then

a catalyst had never been necessary to anyone. How had the idea of such a thing gotten started, then?—And yet, paradoxically, though it did not jar him to give up the idea of the catalyst, his inner conviction about the crystal growing in the nutrient solution being helpful to his talents was stronger than ever.

Suddenly, he felt perfectly sure and certain inside about his ability to pass the test, with or without a catalyst. He put the glasses on; and everything in the room around him went gray.

"Choose," said Waka.

Chaz looked and saw the rice grains spread out on the table top before him.

"Red," he answered.

He stared at the grains. They were all one identical color; but when he looked for those that might be colored red they appeared to stand out to his eye as if they had been individually equipped with flags. Something shouted "red" at him, although his eye refused to see any color difference whatsoever.

This time he did not bother to take the grains one by one and line them up so that later he would be able to tell where he had gone wrong. There was simply no way he could go wrong. He merely brushed away all grains of the wrong color and corralled those he was after in a small pile.

Then he took off the glasses. He had not failed. The red-colored grains were all together in the pile he had made.

Waka sat back in his chair with a heavy sigh. All at once the tension he had shown earlier was drained out of him.

"Well, that's it, then," Waka said. "It's done now."

He reached over and pressed the buttons on his phone. There was a second's hesitation, then a single musical note sounded briefly from the speaker.

"Pritcher Mass Central," said a voice. "Recording your report, Examiner Alexander Waka."

"I've just examined and found qualified a volunteer for

work on the Mass," Waka said. "His name is Charles Roumi Sant, Citizen Number—" He looked at Chaz, raising his eyebrows.

"418657991B," Chaz supplied.

"418657991B," Waka repeated to the phone. "He'll want to leave for the Mass as soon as possible. Meanwhile, he may need immunity from Earth legal procedure."

The phone said nothing for a moment. Then the voice at the other end spoke again.

"We check the name Charles Roumi Sant with the records earlier supplied us by you, on a volunteer tested six times previously without success. We have already signaled Police Central that this man is signed for work on the Mass and no interference with his departure for the Mass must be permitted. Charles Roumi Sant may place himself directly under Mass protection at our Central Headquarters Chicago office, or he may have free time for nine hours until 2000 hours this evening; at which time he will report to the office, ready for departure to the Mass."

"He'll come immediately—"

"No I won't!" Chaz interrupted the examiner. He leaned over to the phone. "This is Charles Sant. I'll be there at 2000 hours."

"Bring no possessions," said the phone. "Nothing from Earth, not even from the sterile areas, is allowed on the Mass."

The connection was broken from the other end. The phone speaker hummed on an open line.

"You're taking a chance," said Waka, punching the phone off.

"I need those nine hours," said Chaz, "to find someone."

"You won't," said Waka.

"I won't?" Chaz leaned forward above the table. "What do you know about it?"

Waka's face twisted unhappily.

"Enough," he said. "Too much. Don't you know once you've gone to the Mass, you can never come back here? You'd have to forget her anyway. Forget her now and make it easier on both of you."

Chaz reached across the table and took hold of the front of his sleeping robe.

"What do you know about Eileen? What do you know about all of this?"

Waka did not move.

"You're an amateur," he said almost contemptuously to Chaz. "Do you think you can scare me? I've been scared by professionals."

Chaz let go of the robe.

"All right," he said grimly. "I think I can put most of it together. You're tied up with the Citadel, too. So you know about what happened to Eileen and me. You know where she is now."

"Not now. I swear I don't," said Waka.

"You're tied up with the Citadel. But the Citadel doesn't want me to go to the Mass; and you've just passed me so that I can go. If you're willing to go against the wishes of the Citadel to pass me, why won't you help me find Eileen?"

Waka slumped in his chair.

"I told you I was a fool," he said, heavily. "But there's a limit to how much a fool any man can be. Now, get out of here."

"No," said Chaz, thoughtfully. "No. Maybe I'll stay here the whole nine hours."

"Get out!" Waka shot to his feet. "Now!"

"All right," Chaz said, without moving. "If you answer a few questions for me, I'll go. Otherwise, not."

"It'll mean the end for you, as well as me, if you're found here by the wrong people," said Waka, a little hoarsely. "Doesn't that matter to you?"

"I'll risk it," said Chaz. "Want to talk?"

Waka sat down again, heavily.

"Oh, damn it, damn it, damn it!" he said helplessly. "What am I going to do?"

"Talk," said Chaz.

"All right." Waka stared at him. "I work for the Citadel as well as the Mass. I passed your name on to the Citadel when you first came to be tested. They did some computer and other checking and came up with the opinion that you on the Mass would be bad medicine for them—don't ask me why, or how. And that's all I know."

"Not quite. What about Eileen?"

"They said they were going to put someone on you," Waka answered sullenly. "It was her, evidently."

"Put someone on me? What does that mean?"

"Someone"—Waka made a helpless gesture with his hand—"someone to find out all about you, to find a weak spot in you, something that would make it easy for them to keep you off the Mass." He still looked at Chaz sullenly. "She's not witch-born for nothing. She must have taken you apart one night and found out what made you tick, so she could report back to the Citadel on it."

"Eileen?" The happenings the night of the party began to glimmer up vaguely into Chaz's consciousness, like the shape of sunken objects dimly seen in deep water. "But she said she didn't have to do anything she didn't want to—and she helped me escape from them. Why help me escape, if she was working on me for the Citadel in the first place?"

"You don't know?" Waka almost sneered. "She's a woman as well as a witch. She fell in love with you—don't ask me why. A witch ought to know better."

"What do you know about witches—and Eileen?"

Waka glared at him for a second, then slumped again.

"I'm a witch," he said, miserably. "What did you think?"

"You?"

A wild suspicion roared like a tornado into Chaz's mind. He took two steps to where Waka sat, reached down and ripped open the blue sleeping robe. Underneath was a padded or inflated device, which fitted around the man's

waist to make him look thirty pounds heavier than the rest
of his body now showed him to be.

"You're the Gray Man!" Chaz exploded. "Answer me! You
are the Gray Man, aren't you?"

Waka drew the robe back around himself with a hiding
motion, as if he would try to escape inside it.

"Leave me alone," he said in a husky whisper. "Get out of
here, and just leave me alone!"

"Oh, no," said Chaz, grimly. "If you're the Gray Man, you
really do know where Eileen is—"

Waka began to laugh, bitterly.

"Know? Me?" he said. "Do you think I'm that important
to the Citadel? You saw how that witch of yours was ready
to push me around and bully me. I'm a go-between, that's
all. I tell the coven what the Citadel wants from them; and
the witches in the coven tell me how much they'll do. I'm
—do you know what I am?"

Tears brimmed unexpectedly in Waka's eyes and slid down
his cheeks.

"I'm a slave!" he said, hoarsely. "I've got paranormal
talents just like you, but not the kind that makes me able to
stand up to anybody. The Citadel owns me—*owns* me!"

He caught himself, shook his head abruptly, swallowed,
and sat up. When he spoke again, his voice was stronger.

"No," he said. "Cancel that. Not quite. They don't quite
own me. Part of me belongs to the Pritcher Mass—and that
part's free of them. Someday the Mass is going to find a new,
clean world for people; and when it does, it's the ordinary
people who'll be left behind and the talented ones who'll
escape. Someday there'll be no Citadel to make a slave out
of anyone like me!"

He got to his feet. Curiously, he seemed to have refound
some of the stature and dignity Chaz had seen in him on the
day in his office when he had told Chaz of his commitment to
the Mass.

"Now," he said, calmly, "if you've got any sense at all,

you'll clear out of here. The Citadel will be sending someone around to check up on me, as soon as they get the record of your call to me, with that credit card you're carrying. By this time they know that card's being used and it means you're using it. So, if you use your head, you'll go right to the Pritcher Mass Chicago office. But in any case, stay clear of me. Because when they come I'll have to tell them you're looking for Eileen Mortvain; and then they'll know where to look for you."

"You're sure you don't know where she is?" Chaz demanded.

Waka shook his head.

"I wouldn't tell you if I did," he said. "But I really don't. They took her right after they took you. I've no idea where."

Chaz turned and went out the door. As it closed behind him, he heard Waka's phone chime with another call.

On the odd chance that that call was from someone involved with the Citadel, he wasted no time. Half an hour later saw him once more on a train from Chicago to the Wisconsin Dells, the passage paid for by the credit card from the hospital attendant, which he still carried.

He arrived at the Dells with seven and a half hours left of his available time before reporting to the Mass Chicago office. He took a P.R.T. car to his own condominium. Happily, the dockage in the condominium basement was empty of travelers, any one of whom might have been a resident who could recognize him. He took the elevator tube.

His attic memory had preserved the number of Eileen's apartment, following that one visit there he had made with her to pick up the wolverine. But when he came to the doorway he remembered, the door itself was standing wide open in locked position, as was customary with tenantless apartments, and all the furniture had been retracted into the floor or the walls, so that the automated hall-cleaning equipment could do maintenance here until a new tenant took over.

He stared into the empty apartment for a moment, then left it and went down the hall to the phone stand and called the building directory.

"Do you have a forwarding address for Ms. Eileen Mortvain, apartment fourteen thirty-three?" he asked.

"I'm sorry," the computerized voice of the directory fluted from the speaker. "No Eileen Mortvain has been listed among the tenants in this building during the past year."

"Check for error, please," said Chaz. "I happen to know she was occupying apartment fourteen thirty-three just a day or two ago, at most."

There was a very slight pause.

"Checked for error. None, sir. No Eileen Mortvain listed in this building during the last year. Previous occupant of fourteen thirty-three was male and departed apartment eighteen days ago."

There was no point in arguing with a machine.

"Thanks," said Chaz automatically, and closed off the phone connection.

He stood thinking for a moment. Then he reached for the phone again and punched the call number of another apartment in the building whose occupant he knew.

"Mrs. Doxeil?" he said, when a female voice answered. "This is Chaz Sant."

"Why yes, Chaz." There was a slight pause before Mrs. Doxeil went on. "We were just wondering if you'd been hurt more than you thought in that train wreck. No one's seen you since—"

"No, I'm fine," he interrupted. "I've just been unusually busy. I wanted to ask you something, though. You know Eileen Mortvain?"

"Eileen Mortvain?"

"Fourteen thirty-three," Chaz said, harshly. "She came to at least one of your condominium parties in the amusement rooms. You must know her. Well, she's moved, it seems; and I was wondering if you knew where, or when she left?"

There was an odd hesitation for a second at the far end; then Mrs. Doxeil's voice answered on an entirely different note.

"Oh yes, dear!" she said. "I'm so sorry; but Eileen didn't want anyone to know she was here. We've been taking care of her in our little place. She's here now; and when she heard me say your name she started waving at me. You're to come down right away."

Chaz sighed with relief.

"I'll be right down," he said.

"We'll be waiting—but, Chaz dear!" cried Mrs. Doxeil's voice over the phone, "if you run into anyone, don't say where you're going!"

"I won't," he said, and broke the connection.

He was turning from the phone rank when a strange noise sounded before him. It was like a low-pitched animal whine, half chewed into words. He heard it clearly, but it was a second before it translated in his head into understandable speech.

"*Lie,*" it said. "*Lie. Chaz not go.*"

He turned. What he saw, crouched next to the wall into such a small shape that he had to look twice to be sure it was actually there in the soft lighting of the hallway, was a wolverine.

"Tillicum?" he said—hardly able to believe that it was Eileen's pet or familiar, he was seeing.

"*Don't go.*" The wolverine's whining was twisted into a mewing sort of speech. "*Eileen not there. Woman lies.*"

"Where then? Where is Eileen?" Chaz lowered his own voice to a whisper just in time, as a door farther down the hall opened and a man came out. However, the man turned away from them, going off toward the elevator tubes.

"*Other place. Sent me—watch for Chaz. Chaz mustn't try find. Must go Mass. Message—go Mass, Chaz.*"

Chaz felt his eyes start to burn as he stared down at the strangely hard-to-see animal.

"Why should I believe you?" he muttered. "I can't trust anyone else."

"*Save Eileen,*" mewed the wolverine. "*Save Eileen by going Mass. No other way. Go now. Or all die—Eileen, Chaz, Tillicum, all.*"

"No," said Chaz, softly but fiercely. "No, I don't think I will. Show me where she is and then I'll go."

"*Can't show.*" Tillicum seemed to shrink even smaller. "*Out of talk now. Last message. Remember spell—think Eileen name but once you are there. On Mass, think Eileen name. Now . . . gone . . .*"

And, unbelievably, Tillicum was in fact gone. Chaz blinked at the spot by the wall where the wolverine had been. For just a moment his sight had blurred, and when it cleared again, the spot had been empty.

In his head, out of his attic memory, Eileen's voice sang again, as he had heard it in his apartment.

> "*Gaest thou down tae Chicago, sae fair?*
> "*Harp at ye, carp at ye, water and wine.*
> "*Thinkst thou my name but once thou art there,*
> "*So shalt thou be a true love o' mine. . . .*"

He had indeed thought her name in Chicago, after he had escaped from the hospital; and now—he faced it finally —he was a true love of hers. Or perhaps he had been in love with her even before that, following that unclear evening in the party rooms. At any rate he cared for her now, as he had never cared for anyone else, and if he had to believe anyone, he would choose to believe her wolverine and its message.

He turned and left the condominium, and returned safely to Chicago, to the Pritcher Mass office there. Ten and a half hours later, he was being lifted into orbit by a ram jet, to rendezvous with an interplanetary ship bound for the Mass with supplies. He was spaceborn after that for twenty days of one-gravity thrust and retro-thrust. At the end of that time and four billion miles from Earth, he was delivered, naked as the first apeman born and still damp from the decontamination shower he had been through, into a passage tunnel leading from the ship to the entrance of the massive metal platform beyond Pluto on which the Pritcher Mass was being built. A tall, slim, dark man in blue coveralls met him and led him to the heavy airlock doors of the entrance itself, now open on the interior darkness of the Mass platform. He was about to proceed into that darkness, when the tall man checked him with a hand on his arm.

"Your last chance," the tall man said. "Stop and think. You can still turn around now, get back on the ship and ride home to Earth."

Chaz looked at him.

"I wouldn't turn back now, even if I wanted to," he answered.

The tall man smiled.

"They all say something like that," he said. "Take notice of the warning, then. . . . You know the line from Dante's *Inferno* that was supposed to be written over the entrance to Hell?

"'. . . *All hope abandon, ye who enter here.*' Canto the Third, isn't it?" said Chaz, delving into the attic to find the line. "Yes, I know it. Why?"

"We've paraphrased it for our own use," said the tall man. "A very important warning for newcomers. Look."

He pointed over the airlock entrance; and Chaz now noticed that there were letters incised in the metal above it. He moved closer until he could read them.

"ALL EARTH ABANDON, YOU WHO JOIN US HERE."

CHAPTER SEVEN

CHAZ STARED at the words, then turned to the slim man.

"What does it mean?" he asked.

"That's something it'll take you a few months here to fully understand," said the other. "You'll be getting a brief version of the answer in a few minutes. Come inside, now."

He led Chaz through the doorway. The heavy outer lock door slid to behind them with a shivering crash of metal; and lights flashed on to show Chaz that they stood in the lock itself, a space at least the size of Waka's apartment with the two rooms of it thrown into one. A sudden tug of nearly 1G on his body surprised him; and then he remembered that the Mass had space to spare—even enough to provide a room for the generators necessary to produce a continuous gravity field. Airsuits hung on a rack along one wall to Chaz's left. Along the wall to his right was another rack, holding blue coveralls. Between both walls, at the far end, was the inner lock door, which was now beginning to open.

"Get dressed," said the slim man, waving at the rack of coveralls. Chaz obeyed, and when he finished found the other ready with a hand outstretched to him. "By the way, I'm Jai Losser, the Assistant Director on the Mass. Sorry, but our rule is we don't even give our names outside that door."

Chaz shook hands.

"Charles Roumi Sant," he said.

"Oh, I know your name," Jai laughed. He had a pleasant laugh and his thin face lit up with good humor. "We've got a heavy dossier on you, phoned over from the supply ship with other mail and information when she was docking. I'm going to take you now to meet the Director, Lebdell Marti. He'll give you your initial briefing. Know where you are right now, on the Mass?"

"I've seen diagrams," answered Chaz.

In fact, those diagrams had been in his mind more than once on the twenty-day trip here. They had shown the Pritcher Mass as a unit made up of three parts. One part was an asteroid-like chunk of granitic rock about twelve by eight miles, roughly the shape of an egg with one bulging end. Covering half of the surface of this rock was a huge steel deck, some fourteen stories thick. From the upper surface of this deck rose what looked like an ill-assorted forest of antennae; steel masts of heights varying from a hundred meters to over a kilometer. Between the masts, steel cables were looped at intervals, and small power lifts or cable cars moved Mass workers up the masts or across the cables.

Surrounding and extending beyond the masts and cables was something that did not show to the human eye or to any physical instruments—the Mass, itself. In the diagrams Chaz had seen, the illustrators had rendered it transparently in the shape of an enormous shadowy construction crane; although no one was supposed to take this as a serious rendering of its actual form—any more than anyone could seriously imagine a physical crane that could swing its shovel across light years of distance to touch the surface of a distant planet.

"Third level, West End, aren't we?" Chaz asked. "West" was, of course, a convenience term. For purposes of direction on the Mass itself, one end of the platform had arbitrarily been labeled "West," the other "East." "Up" would be in the direction of the deck surface overhead.

"That's right," said Jai. He had a soft, bass voice. "And we go in to Centerpoint to the Director's office."

He led the way out of the lock into a somewhat larger room, half filled with fork-lift trucks and other machinery for transferring cargo. Some of these were already trundling toward the lock on automatic as the two men left it.

"It'll take thirty hours or so to get all the supplies off and the ship ready to leave again," said Jai, as they went through swinging metal doors at the far end of the machinery room into a wide corridor with a double moving-belt walkway both going and coming along its floor. Jai led the way on to the belt and it carried them off down the brightly lighted, metal-walled corridor. "This is our storage area. First level."

"Living and work levels are above us?" Chaz said, as they passed an open doorway and he looked in to see a warehouse-like space stacked with large cartons on pallets.

"Fourth to sixth levels and eighth to fourteenth are quarters and work areas," answered Jai. "Seventh level is all office—administrative. Originally living quarters for the administrative people—the non-talented—were to be on seven, too; but it was felt after a while that this made for an emotional division among the people here. So now the administrators have apartments with the rest of us."

"Us?" Chaz looked sideways at the other man. "I thought you said you were the Assistant Director?"

"I am," Jai said. "But I'm also a worker on the Mass. The workers have to be represented among the administrative staff, too. Leb—the Director, now—is a non-worker." He smiled a little at Chaz. "We tend to talk about people here as divided into workers and non-workers, rather than talented and non-talented. It is a little more courteous to those who don't have the ability to work on the Mass."

Chaz nodded. There was a curious emotional stirring inside him. He had thought about working on the Mass for so long that he had believed that he took it for granted. He had not expected to find himself unusually excited simply by actually being here. But he found he was; in fact, remarkably so; and it was hard to believe that this geared-up sensation in him was only self-excitement.

"I feel hyped-up," he said to Jai, on impulse. He did not usually talk about himself; but Jai had an aura about him that encouraged friendship and confidences. "Funny feeling —like being too close to a static generator and having my hair standing on end. Only it's my nerves, not my hair, that're standing up straight and quivering."

Jai nodded soberly.

"You'll get used to it," he said. "That's one reason we know the Mass is there, even if we can't see it, feel it, or measure it—that feeling you mention. Even the non-workers feel it. In spite of the fact they aren't sensitive to anything else about it."

"You mean people with no talent can *feel* the Mass, up there?" Chaz glanced ceilingward. "That's sort of a contradiction in terms, isn't it?"

Jai shrugged again.

"Nobody can explain it," he said. "But then, just about everything we're doing here is done on blind faith, anyway. We try something and it works. Did you ever stop to think that the Mass we're building here may be a piece of psychic machinery that was never intended to do the thing we're building it for?"

"You mean it might not work?"

"I mean," said Jai, "it might work, but only as a side issue. As if we were building an aircraft so that we could plow a field by taxiing up and down with a plow blade dragging behind our tail section. Remember, no one really knows what

...e Mass is. All we have is Jim Pritcher's theory that it's a means of surveying distant worlds; and Pritcher died before work out here was even started."

"I know," said Chaz. He glanced appraisingly at the Assistant Director. What Jai had just been talking about was a strange sort of idea to throw at a newcomer who had just arrived for work on the Mass. Unless the other had been fishing for some unusual, unguarded response from Chaz.

They went on down the corridor and took an elevator tube upward to the seventh level. Getting off at the seventh level, they went East a short distance down another corridor and turned in through an opaque door into a small outer office where a tiny, but startlingly beautiful, black-haired girl, looking like a marble and ebony figurine, sat at a communications board talking with someone who seemed to be the cargo officer aboard the supply ship Chaz had just left.

". . . *thirty-five hundred units, K74941,*" she was saying as they came in. She looked up and gave them a wave before going back to her board. "*Check. To Bay M, pallet A4*—go right in, Jai. He's waiting for you both—*nineteen hundred units J44, sleeved. To Bay 3, pallets N3 and N4 . . .*"

Jai led Chaz on past her through a further door. They came into a somewhat larger room, brown-carpeted, dominated by a large desk complex of communicating and computer reference equipment. Seated in the midst of the complex was a large, middle-aged, gray-skinned man full of brisk and nervous movements.

"Oh, Jai—Mr. Sant. Come in—pull up some chairs." Lebdell Marti had a hard baritone voice, with a faint French accent. "Be with you in a moment. . . . Ethrya?"

He had spoken into the grille of his communicating equipment. The voice of the living figurine in the outer office answered.

"Yes, Leb?"

"Give me about ten–fifteen minutes of non-interruption. No more, though. Or I'll never catch up."

"Right. I'll call you in fifteen minutes, then."

"Thanks." Lebdell Marti sat back in his chair, the spring back creaking briefly as it gave with his weight. Then he got to his feet and offered his hand to Chaz, who shook it. "Welcome."

They all sat down; and Marti rummaged among his equipment to come up with a thick stack of yellow message sheets.

"Your dossier," he said, holding the stack up briefly for Chaz to see, then dropping it back down on a desk surface of his complex. "No great surprises in it, as far as I can see. All our workers on the Mass are strong individualists; and I see you're no exception. How do you feel about being here at last?"

"Good," said Chaz.

Marti nodded.

"That's the answer we expect," he said. His chair creaked again as he settled back. "Jai pointed out to you the message over the airlock on the way in? Good. Because we take those words very seriously here, for a number of reasons. You'll be learning more about that as you get settled in here; but basically it adds up to the fact that work with a psychic piece of machinery like the Mass requires an essentially artistic sort of commitment. The Mass has to be everything to each one of us. Everything. And that means any commitment to Earth has got to be pushed out of our heads completely. Now . . . how much do you know about the Mass?"

"I've read what's in the libraries back on Earth about it."

"Yes," Marti said. "Well, there's a sort of standard briefing that I give to every new worker who joins us here. Most of it you've probably read or heard already; but we like to make sure that any misconceptions on the part of our incoming people are cleared up at the start. Just what do you know."

"The Mass was James Pritcher's idea," said Chaz, "according to what I learned—although it was just a theoretical notion to him. As I understand it, he died without thinking anyone would ever actually try to build it."

Marti nodded.

"Go on," he said.

"Well, that's all there is to it, isn't it?" Chaz said. "Pritcher was a research psychologist studying in the paranormal and extrasensory fields. He postulated that while no paranormal talent was ever completely dependable, that a number of people who had demonstrated abilities of that kind, working together, might complement each other enough so that they would be able to create a psychic construct—in essence, a piece of non-material machinery. And possibly that kind of machinery could do what material machinery couldn't, because of the physical limitations on material substances. For example, maybe we could build a piece of psychic machinery that could search out and actually contact the surfaces of worlds light years from the Solar System—which is exactly what the Mass is being built to do."

"Exactly," murmured Jai. Chaz glanced at the tall man, remembering Jai's words about the Mass possibly being something other than it was intended to be.

"That's right—is it, exactly?" echoed Marti, behind the complex. "Because the truth is, Charles—"

"Chaz, I'm usually called," Chaz said.

"Chaz—when we get right down to it, we really don't know what we're building here. The Mass is non-material; but it's also something else. It's *subjective*. It's like a work of art, a piece of music, a painting, a novel—the abilities in our workers that create it are more responsive to their subconscious than to their conscious. We may be building here something that only seems to be what our conscious minds desire—a means of discovering and reaching some new world our race can emigrate to. Actually it may turn out to be something entirely different that we desire—with a desire that's been buried in the deep back of our heads, all along."

"The Mass may not work, then, you mean?" Chaz said.

"That's right," said Marti. "It might not work. Or it might work wrong. We only know we're building anything at all, because of the feedback—the *feel* of the presence of the Mass. You've already sensed that, yourself?"

Chaz nodded.

"So, maybe we're just in the position of a group of clever savages," Marti said, "fitting together parts of a machine we don't understand on a sort of jigsaw puzzle basis, a machine that may end up doing nothing, or blowing up in our faces. Of course, we've come a long way in the last fifty years. We realize nowadays that paranormal or psychic—whatever you want to call them—abilities do exist in certain people; even if they can't be measured, dealt with, or used according to any rules we know. But a lot of that distance we've come has also been downhill. For one thing—the most important thing—we managed to foul our nest back on Earth, until now it's unlivable. Not only that, but we went right on making it unlivable even back when there was still time to save it, in spite of the fact we knew better. The people still on Earth may last another fifty, or another five hundred, years; but they're headed for extinction eventually by processes our great-grandparents instigated. In short, as we all know, humanity on Earth is under a death sentence. And a race under death sentence could have some pretty twisted and powerful, subconscious drives in its individuals; even in individuals with psychic talents building something like the Pritcher Mass."

Marti stopped speaking; and sat staring at Chaz. Chaz waited, and when the other still sat silent, spoke up himself.

"You want me to say something to that?" he asked.

"I do," replied Marti.

"All right," said Chaz. "Even if what you say is true, I don't see how it matters a damn. The Mass is the only thing we've come up with. We're going to build it anyway. So why worry about it? Since we've got no choice but to plug ahead and build it anyway, let's get on with that, and not worry about the details."

"All right," said Marti. "But what if the subconscious details in one worker's mind can mess us all up? What if something like that keeps the Mass from coming out the way it should, or working when done?"

"Is there any real evidence that could happen?" Chaz asked.

"Some," said Marti, dryly. "We've had some odd reactions here and there among the workers themselves. You may run across some in yourself in the next minutes—or few months, so I won't describe them to you. The fact remains, as I kept trying to impress on you, that we really don't know what we're creating; and in any case we've got no experience in this type of psychic creation. All we can do, as you say, is keep on building. But we can take one precaution."

Chaz lifted his eyebrows questioningly.

"We can try to get the greatest possible concentration by our workers on the conscious aim we have for the Mass," Marti said. "That's why the legend was over the airlock when you came in. That's why I'm talking to you now about this. Whatever memories or associations you've got in your mind about Earth, forget them. Now, put them out of your mind in every way you can. If they crop up unexpectedly, cut them down utterly and quickly. Concentrate on the Mass, on this place here, on your co-workers and on the world we hope to find. Forget Earth and everyone on it. They're already dead as far as you're concerned. You may not be one of those who'll emigrate to the new world when we find it—in fact the odds are against any of us here being that lucky—but you're never going back to Earth again. We won't even send your body back, if you die. Keep that in mind, and meditate on it."

Meditate . . . "*Thinkst thou my name but once thou art there . . .*" The ghost of a song fragment sounded unbidden in the back of Chaz's mind. Eileen . . . Marti was standing up and extending his hand. Chaz rose and shook hands with the Director again.

"All right," said Marti. "Jai will get you started. Good luck."

"Thanks," said Chaz.

He followed Jai out the door. They passed through the outer office where Ethrya was still reciting numbers and directions into her communications equipment. They left and took an elevator tube up.

"Want to see your quarters now?" Jai asked, as they floated upward on the elevator disk. "Or would you rather take a look at the Mass, first?"

"The Mass, of course—" Chaz stared at the slim man. "You mean I can go to it right away, like this?"

"That's right," Jai smiled. "For that matter, you could try to go to work right away, if you wanted to. But I'd advise against it. It's better to have some experience of what it feels like up there on top, before you try doing anything about it."

"Go to work?" Chaz decided that the other man was serious. "How could I go to work? I don't even know what I'm supposed to do, much less how to do it."

"Well," said Jai, as the various levels slipped by outside the transparent tube of the elevator shaft, "those are things no one can help you with. You're going to have to work them out for yourself. You see, they're different for everyone who works on the Mass. Everyone has a different experience up there; and each person has to find out how to work with it in his own way. As Leb said—this is creative work, like painting, composing, or writing. No one can teach you how to do it."

"How do I learn, then?"

"You fumble around until you teach yourself, somehow." Jai shrugged. "You might just possibly learn how the minute you set foot on the deck. But if you're still trying three months from now that'll be closer to the average experience."

"There must be something you can tell me," Chaz said. The unusual nervous excitement he had felt from the moment he had arrived was building inside him to new peaks, as their disk carried them closer and closer to the Mass itself.

Jai shook his head.

"You'll find out how it is, once you've discovered your own way of working with the Mass," he said. "You'll know how you do it, then, but what you know won't be anything you can explain to anyone else. The best tip I can give you is not to push. Relax and let what happens, happen. You can't force yourself to learn, you know. You just have to go along with your own reactions and emotions until you find yourself taking hold instinctively.

Their disk stopped. Above them the tube ended in ceiling. Jai led Chaz from it out into a very large room filled with construction equipment; and the two of them got into airsuits from a rack near a further elevator.

Suited, they took the further elevator up through the ceiling overhead. Their ride ended in a small windowless building with an airlock.

"Brace yourself," said Jai to Chaz over the suit phones, and led the way out of the airlock.

Chaz was unclear as to how he might have been supposed to brace himself; but it turned out that this did not matter. No matter how he might have tried to prepare himself for what he encountered on the outside, airless deck, he realized later, it would not have helped.

He stepped into a great metal plain roofed with a dome of brilliant stars seemingly upheld by the faintly lighted, gleaming pillars of the metal masts. It was as he had seen it pictured in books. But the ghostly shape of a great construction crane was not superimposed on it. Instead, his imagination saw the elevator cages on the masts and the cars on the metal cables as part of his favorite image of seed crystals on threads immersed in a nutrient solution. For a moment, almost, he convinced himself he saw the Mass itself, like a great, red potassium ferrocyanide crystal, growing in the midst of all this.

"This way," Jai's voice was saying in his earphones; and Jai's grip on his airsuited arm was leading him to the base of the nearest mast, into a metal elevator cage there barely big enough to hold them both at the same time.

They entered the cage. Jai's gloved hands touched a bank of controls, and the cage began to slide swiftly and silently up the mast. As the deck dropped away beneath them, the excitement in Chaz, the perception of an additional dimension, shot up toward unbearability. All at once it seemed they were out of sight of the deck, high among the stars and the masts, with the softly-lit silver cables looping between them; and without warning the whole impact of the Mass came crashing in upon Chaz at once.

It poured over and through him like a tidal flood. Suddenly, the whole universe seemed to touch him at once; and he was swept away and drowning in a depthless sadness; a sadness so deep he would not have believed it was possible. It cascaded over him like the silent but deafening music of some great, inconceivable orchestra, each note setting up a sympathetic vibration in every cell of his body.

Consciousness began to leave him under the emotional assault. He was vaguely aware of slumping, of being caught by Jai and upheld as the other man reached out with one hand to slap the control panel of the cage. They reversed their motion, rocking back down the mast. But the silent orchestra pursued them, thundering all about and through Chaz, shredding his feelings with great, voiceless chords.

An unbearable sadness for all of mankind overwhelmed him—agony for all its bright rise, its foolish errors that had led to its present failure, and its stumbling, falling, plunging down now toward extinction . . .

Sorrow racked him—for Earth, for his people, for everything he had known and loved.

Eileen . . . Eileen Mortvain . . .

—And the great silent orchestra picked up the name, roaring into the melody that went with the words he was remembering:

"*Thinkst thou my name but once thou art there . . .*"

"Eileen," he muttered, upheld by Jai. "Eileen . . ."

"*Chaz?*" Out of the orchestra sound, out of the Mass, the unimaginable dimension of the universe he had just discovered, and the sorrow and tragedy of the murdered Earth, he heard her voice calling.

". . . *Chaz? Are you there? Can you hear me? Chaz . . . ?*"

CHAPTER EIGHT

HE OPENED his eyes, wondering where he was. Then he recognized the white-paneled ceiling two meters above him as the ceiling of the bedroom in the spacious quarters that had been assigned him at the Mass. It had been five days now since his arrival and he was not yet accustomed to having three large, high-ceilinged rooms all to himself.

He became conscious, almost in the same moment as that in which he identified the ceiling, of an additional weight sharing the mattress on which he lay. Away out here on the Mass, water beds were impractical; and the spring mattresses carried signals once the sleeper got used to them. He turned his head and saw Ethrya perched on the edge of his bed.

She was smiling down at him. It had not occurred to him, here on the Mass, to lock his apartment door, so that there was no mystery about how she could be here. Why, was something else again.

"You're awake at last," she said.

"What's up?" he asked.

"I'm about to go out on the Mass on one of my own work shifts there," she answered. "Leb suggested you might want to go along with me. Sometimes it helps someone new if they spend a shift outside with another person who's already found how to work with the Mass."

"Oh," he said.

She sat on the edge of the bed level with his right hip as he lay on his back; and she was only inches from him. Since that first moment in which he had heard Eileen's voice out on the Mass, he had not been able to achieve any contact with Eileen again; but she had been in his mind constantly. Nonetheless—for all of Eileen—to come up out of drowsy sleep and find a startlingly beautiful small woman close beside him was to experience an unavoidable, instinctive response.

Even seen this close up, Ethrya's beauty was flawless. She wore coveralls as just about everyone did, on the Mass. But those she was wearing at the moment were white, and they fitted her very well. The somewhat stiff material pressed close to her at points, but stood away from her at others, with a faintly starched look. So that looking at her, it was easy to imagine her body moving inside the clothing. The coveralls were open at the throat and above the collar her black hair set off the ivory of her skin, giving her face a cameo look. There was a faint, clean smell to her.

"Were you married?" she asked Chaz now.

He shook his head, watching her.

"Oh?" she said. "I wondered. Jai said you spoke the name of some woman that first day when you collapsed up top. Who was it, if it wasn't a wife?"

Instinctively, through remnants of sleep that still fogged his mind, his early years of experience at defending himself among his aunt and cousins shouted a warning. Without pausing to search out the reasons for it, he lied immediately, smoothly, and convincingly.

"My aunt," he said. "She raised me after my father died. My mother was already dead."

She stared down into his face for a moment.

"Well," she said. "An aunt. That dossier Leb got on you said something about you being a loner. But I didn't think it was that serious."

She slipped off the bed and stood up. There was no doubt about the way she did it that she was physically taking herself away from him. And yet, she was still within long arm's reach. Chaz had a sudden strong impulse to reach out and haul her back; and only the same instinct that had spoken earlier—this time, however, telling him that doing so would be to do exactly what she wanted from him—stopped him.

Instead, he lay there and looked at her.

"Anybody entitled to read that dossier of mine, are they?" he asked.

"Of course not," she said. "Only Leb. But I work in the office part of the time. I thought I'd take a look." She looked down at him for a second, smiling faintly. "How about it? Want to meet me in the dining area in about twenty minutes and we'll go out on the Mass together?"

"Fine," he said. "Thanks."

"Don't mention it."

She turned and walked out. She managed to make a work of art even out of that.

Left alone, Chaz levered himself out of bed, showered—a cold shower—and dressed. Wearing gray coveralls, he took the elevator up to third level to the dining area. Ethrya was waiting for him at one of the small tables.

"Better eat something, if you haven't in the last few hours, before we go up," she said.

"Breakfast," he agreed, sitting down. "How about you?"

"I had lunch an hour ago," Ethrya answered. Sleeping and eating and working schedules were highly individual on the Mass. "I'll just sit here and keep you company."

He got his tray of food from the disposer and dug into it.

Ethrya sat chatting about work on the Mass. Upstairs here, in public, there were none of the earlier signals of sex wafting from her. She was cheerful, brisk, and impersonal—and the contrast with the way she had appeared down in his bedroom made her more enticing than ever. Chaz concentrated on being just as friendly and brisk.

"You aren't going to be able to work with the Mass," she said, "until you've become able to sense its pattern. It does have a pattern, you know. The fact that no two of the workers describe it the same way makes no difference. The pattern's there—and once you can feel it, you'll be ready to start figuring out what needs to be added to it to make it whole. Once you fully conceive of an addition you'll find it's been added to the Mass—not only in the pattern as you see it, but in the pattern of everyone else who's working on it."

Chaz thought of his own image of a nutrient solution with a great red crystal growing in it. He swallowed a mouthful of omelet.

"All subjective, then?" he asked.

"Very subjective," she said.

He managed another mouthful, while mentally debating something he wanted to ask her. He decided to ask it.

"How do you see the Mass?" he asked.

"Like an enormous bear," she answered promptly. "A friendly bear—white, like a polar bear. He's sitting up the way bears do. Maybe you've seen them do it in zoos. They sit with their back up straight and their hind legs straight out before them. He sits like that among the stars, half as big as the universe; and he stretches out one foreleg straight from the shoulder, pointing at whatever I want. All I have to do is walk out along that foreleg to get to any place this side of infinity."

Chaz watched her as she talked.

"Have you?" he asked.

"I came close, once," she answered. "There's a number of us who've had glimpses of the kind of world we're looking for. The trouble is, my bear isn't finished, yet; and until he's finished, he isn't strong enough to keep that foreleg held out straight while I locate the world he's helped me get to. Or, at least, that's the shape the problem takes for me, when I work upstairs."

"A bear," he said, finishing up the omelet. "That's strange. I thought everyone would think of the Mass as something mechanical."

"A number of the workers see it as something alive," Ethrya said. "Most of the women here—what there are of them."

He glanced at her curiously.

"You sound a little old-fashioned," he said. "I thought all that about equality got settled in the last century?"

"Look around you," she said; "the men outnumber us five to one up here."

"Maybe that's the way the talent for chain-perception distributes itself?"

"You know better. The old system still operates. There's plenty of women with the talent to work here," Ethrya's dark eyes glittered, "but they've had the guts choked out of them. They'd rather stay where they are and play their little witch games—even if Earth is a dead end."

Chaz carefully lifted his coffee cup and drank from it without looking at her, and carefully put the cup down. Then he looked at her; and her face was perfectly pleasant and serene.

"You'd know more about it than I would," he said.

"I would, indeed," she said, cheerfully. "Now, are you ready for the Mass?"

He nodded. They got up, left the dining area, and took the elevator to the top level. Ten minutes later they were out on the deck in their airsuits, walking clumsily side by side toward a cage at the foot of one of the masts.

"Keep your suit phone open on my circuit," her voice said in his earphones. "That way I'll be able to hear anything you

say. Usually, if people begin to hallucinate here on the Mass,
they talk or make some kind of sounds that gives it away."

"Hallucinate?" he echoed, as they fitted themselves into
the cage and began to rise up the mast. "Is that supposed to
be what happened to me the first day?"

"Of course," she said. "What else?"

"I don't know," he said. "I just didn't think of it as a hallucination."

"Oh, yes," she said. "It happens all the time, even after
you've learned how to work up top. You were just lucky it
wasn't a bad one—like the universe going all twisted and
crazy. In a strict sense, the Mass isn't even real, you know.
Any characteristics it has are things our minds give it. It's all
subjective around here. You start getting hallucinations that
are really bad and Leb'll have to take you off the work up
here."

"I see," he answered.

"Don't worry about it. How do you feel now?"

"I don't feel anything," he said. It was true. Since that first
day he had been back up on the Mass a half dozen times, and
each time there had been no more to it than clumping around
in an airsuit and riding mast elevator cages and cable cars
through airless space.

"If you start to feel anything, let me know," she told him.
"Actually, there's two things here. The Mass itself and the
force of the Mass. So, you do want to feel something—the
Mass-force pushing against you. But you want to control
that push, meter it down to a force you can handle, so it
doesn't overwhelm you the way it did the first time."

Their cage stopped at a cable. They got out and trans-
ferred to a cable car, which began to slide out along the cable
into a void in which they seemed all but surrounded by stars.

"What would happen if you learned how to manage the
full force without metering it down to a something smaller?"
he asked.

"You couldn't take it," her voice answered within his helmet. "We've had a few people who couldn't learn how to meter it down and they all collapsed, eventually. That's when the hallucinations start getting bad, when the full flow can't be controlled. You can blow your mind out, then."

Chaz stowed that information away in his mental attic, together with a perceptible grain of salt. He would discover his own truths about the Mass, he decided, for himself and at first hand.

"The thing is"—the purely human voice of Ethrya sounded tiny and unnatural, coming over the earphones of Chaz's suit—"to take it as gently as possible. Just sit back and let the force of the Mass seep into you, if that's the word. How do you feel now?"

"Fine," said Chaz.

"Good." She stopped the cage in mid-cable. "I'm ready to go to work now. If you pick up any feeling from me, or from the Mass-force, speak up. Maybe I can help you with it—or maybe not. But check anyway."

"All right," Chaz said.

He sat back in his airsuit. Silence fell. Beside him, Ethrya was equally silent. He wondered if she was already walking out along the outstretched forelimb of her enormous bear. How long would it take her, in her mind, to walk the light years of distance from his shoulder to wherever she believed he was pointing?

Chaz tried to put his mind on the Mass; but the female presence of Ethrya alongside him interfered, in spite of the double wall of airsuiting between them. His mind went back to Eileen. It had been no hallucination, that voice of hers he had heard, on his first day here. He might be open to argument on other points about the Mass, but on that one he had no doubt. He and Eileen had been in contact for at least a few seconds, thanks to the Mass; and what had been done once could be done again.

. . .That is, if he could only get once more into touch with the Mass itself. A small cold fear stirred inside him. The pos-

sibility of hallucinations did not worry him; but Jai had
talked of three months or more of effort before Chaz might
learn to work with the Mass. How much time would they actually be willing to give to learn? Somewhere . . . he began
to search through the attic of his memory . . . he had read
something about those who after six months or so could not
learn to work. They were not sent back to Earth. Like those
Ethrya had been talking about, who could not stand up emotionally or mentally to contact with the Mass, they were
kept on as administrative personnel. But administrative personnel were never allowed up here on the deck.

The earphones of his suit spoke suddenly. But it was not a
call for him. It was Lebdell Marti, speaking to Ethrya—he
heard the call only because of the open channel between the
phones of his suit and hers.

"Ethrya? This is Leb. Are you up on the Mass?"

"Hello?" She answered immediately, almost as if she had
been waiting for the call, instead of out somewhere on the
forelimb of her bear. "What is it, Leb? I'm on the Mass with
Chaz Sant. I thought it might help him if I took him out in
partnership for a try."

Marti did not speak for a second.

"I see," he said then. "Well, I'm sorry to interrupt; but
some of those supplies from the ship last week must have
gotten stored in the wrong place. Either that, or they weren't
sent. Can you break off and come down to the office to help
me find out which?"

"I'll be right down." There was a faint click in the earphones as Marti broke contact. The helmet of Ethrya's airsuit turned toward Chaz in the cable car. "Sorry, Chaz. You're
going in, too?"

She had already touched the controls of the cable car and
it was gliding along the silver catenary curve of the cable toward the nearest mast.

"No," said Chaz. "As long as I'm suited-up anyway, I think
I'll stay up here a bit and go on trying."

"Whatever you want." The car touched the mast and stopped. She got out. "Better keep your phones open on the general channel, though. If you should have another hallucination, you want somebody to hear you and get you down."

"Right," he said, and watched her go. The cage she entered slid down the mast below him to the deck and he saw her shrunken, foreshortened, airsuited figure go across the deck to the nearest elevator housing.

Left alone, high on the mast, he tongued his phone over to the general channel. He heard the hum of its particular carrier wave tone, and felt a sudden, gentle coolness against the skin inside his right elbow. For a second, he was merely puzzled—and then instinct hit the panic button.

He flipped his phone off the general channel with his tongue, but the damage was already done. Something had already started to take hold of his mind—something that was not the Mass, but a thing sick and chemical.

"Help!" he thought—and for all he knew, shouted inside his airsuit helmet. He reached out for aid in all directions—to the attic of his memory, to his own talent, to the Mass itself. . . . "Eileen! Eileen, help me! They've . . ."

His mind and voice stumbled at the enormity of what someone had done to him. He felt his consciousness begin to twist into nightmare.

"*Chaz! Is it you? Are you there?*"

"Eileen," he mumbled. "I've been drugged. I'm up on the Mass and they've drugged me . . ."

"*Oh, Chaz! Hold on. Hold on to contact with me. This time I won't lose you—*"

"No use," he muttered. She was still talking to him; but her voice was becoming fainter as the nightmare crowded in. "Starting to drift. Need help. Need Mass . . ."

He thought longingly, with the little spark of sanity that was still in him, of the great silent symphony he had heard the first time he had been out here. Nothing could twist that rush of unconquerable majesty. Only, he could not find it now. He could not feel it when he needed it. . . .

But he could. His feeling for Eileen had triggered his demand for contact with it. After that, the thrust of his desperation was sufficient. Far off through the gibbering craziness that had surrounded him and was carrying him away, he heard its first notes; the music of the Mass-force. It was coming. And there was nothing that could stand before it and bar its way.

CHAPTER NINE

IT CAME like an iron-shod giant striding through a nest of snakes. It came like all the winds of all the stars blowing at once upon the smog and fog and illness of little Earth. It came like the turning wheel of the universe itself, descending upon the eggshell of a merely man-made prison.

The voice of the Mass, unbarred, unmetered, roared through Chaz's body and mind as it had roared once before; and the effect of the drug was swallowed, quenched, and drowned utterly. Like a leaf in a tornado—but a clean leaf, now—Chaz was snatched up and whirled away.

For a while he let the Mass-voice fling him where it would. But, gradually, the memory of Eileen speaking to him returned, along with the desire and need to hear her speak again; and for the first time he began to try to ride the tornadic force that had saved him.

It was like being an eagle whose wings had been bound from birth, and who was only now learning at last to soar in

the heart of a storm. There was no teacher but instinct; no
guide but the waking of dormant reflexes; but slowly these
two took over. It was what the faculty of chain-perception
had been meant to be all along—but what Chaz had not
really understood it to mean until now: The true definition
of the choosing by which useless and wrong actions were
discarded, and the useful and true caught, to be linked together into a cable reaching to a desired conclusion.

So, finally, he came to control the force of the Mass—or at
least, close enough to control so that he was able to form
his own image of it. That image was of a massive dark mountain of whirling wind, emerging from the great crystal he
imagined growing in the nutrient solution of the Mass itself.
He had ridden the various currents of that wind now, safely
up from its base where he might have been blown to tatters,
or whirled away forever; and he still had a far way to climb
to its peak. But the distance yet to go did not matter. He was
on the way; and by making use of as much of the Mass-force
as he already controlled, he could reach Eileen easily.

He rode the force, reaching out with his concern for her.

"Eileen?" he called.

"*You're back! Chaz, are you all right?*"

He laughed with the exultation of riding the Mass-force.

"I am now," he said. "I just got a good grip on the horse
I'm riding here. It almost bucked me off at first."

"*What? I don't understand you.*"

"Didn't you ever read those old Western— Never mind," he
said. "It doesn't matter. What matters is, we're back in
touch."

"*But what happened, Chaz? You were in trouble, weren't
you?*"

"Somebody rigged the airsuit I'm wearing out on the Mass,
right now. It gave me a shot of some hallucinogen. But the
Mass helped me counteract it. I'm fine. What about you?
Where are you, Eileen?"

"In the Citadel. But I'm all right too. They're even going to let me go, soon, they say."

"In the Citadel? You mean it's a place? I thought it was an organization."

"It's both. An organization first, and a place second, even if the place is—well, never mind that, now. I've got something I want to tell you, Chaz—"

"But just a minute. What did you start to say just now about the Citadel, the place? Where is it, anyway? What's it like? Finish what you started to tell me about it."

"I meant—even if it is something like a real citadel. I mean, a fortress. The name of it is the Embry Tower; and it looks like any big condominium-office building from the outside. Inside, it's different. And it's somewhere in the Chicago area, I think."

"Where's Tillicum? Is the wolverine there with you? Have they got you locked up, or what?"

"No, Tillicum's not here," her voice answered. "I could have him if I wanted him, but I don't. I've given him to another witch in my coven, for now. As for me, I'm out. I said they were going to let me go. Now, Chaz, listen. Let me talk. This is important."

"You're what's important," he said. "Anything else comes second—"

"No, I mean it. I want you to know about me and the Citadel. Look, I told you the truth. I don't belong to it. But all the members of our coven did deal with it. The Citadel could help us stay hidden and be left alone by other people. We were always used to dealing with some kind of organization—well, never mind that. The thing is, the Citadel made a deal with me to do something for them. I was to move into your condominium, get to meet you, and try to block your talent with mine—put a hex on it, in the old terms—when you tried to use it to pass the test for work on the Mass."

"You?" he said.

"Yes—I'm sorry, Chaz. I'm so sorry; but I didn't know . . .

*anything about you, then. It wasn't until I arranged to meet
you that night in the party rooms that I began to understand
you, and what you believed in. You weren't drunk that night,
really. I made you drunk—and not even with craft, but with
drugs. I wanted you to talk; because the more you told me,
the more hold I'd have on your talent. Dear Chaz, of course
you didn't know about me, then; but you shouldn't even
tell a witch your name.—Much less tell her everything you
believe in."*

"It didn't do any harm," Chaz said. "I'm here on the Mass,
anyway."

"But I meant harm—then," she answered. *"I wasn't any
different from the people in the Citadel; I was just as deadly
toward you as that sick, exiled man the Citadel must have
bribed to blow up your train when I couldn't stop you. But
never mind that. What I want you to know is that you didn't
get away from the Citadel just because you were shipped out
to the Mass. There're Citadel people there, too."*

"After what just happened," he said grimly, "you don't
have to tell me. Who are they, out here; and what is the Citadel, anyway? Everybody talks about it as if it was a name and
nothing else."

"That's all it is," she said. *"A name—for the few people on
top of things, with a lot of power and a lot of connections.
Does it really even matter who they are? All through the
centuries there've always been some like them, who took advantage of other people to get what they wanted themselves.
The Gray Man's the only one I know, and he can't be too
important. But there are others out there on the Mass."*

"What do they want from us, anyway?" he said. "What do
they want from me? I've never bothered them."

"Except by wanting to work on the Mass."

"Lots of people want to work on the Mass. What happened? Did I take a job they wanted for one of their own
people?"

"No," she said. *"But you're different. You're dangerous to* them. I can't explain too well why, Chaz. But the Citadel has people with paranormal talents, and it's got computers. It can put the two together to get a rough forecast of what any person might do to its plans—particularly any person under captive conditions, the way you all are, out there on the Mass. They run a check automatically on anyone who tries to qualify for work on the Mass."

"Why? What's the Mass to them?" he demanded. "There's no market for illegal goods and services here, is there?"

"Of course not. But they want the Mass for themselves—what did you expect? They want to be the people, or among the people, who get a chance to emigrate to a clean world, if the Mass can find one."

"And they think I'm going to stop them? What're they afraid of?" A wild thought struck him suddenly. "Eileen—do I have some special paranormal talent I don't know anything about? Or more talent than anyone else—something like that?"

"Dear Chaz . . ." she said, "you do have talent, but nothing like that. If my talent hadn't been greater than yours, for instance, I couldn't have blocked you out on those early tests you took. It isn't paranormal abilities that make you dangerous to them. It's the way the linked events work in a probability chain—the very thing chain-perception discovers. The alternatives anyone perceives are determined by his own way of looking at the universe—his own attitudes. For some reason, your attitudes are different from other people's. All wrong—or all right—or something. From the Citadel's standpoint they could be all wrong; and the Citadel didn't want to take the chance."

"The man you call the Gray Man was my examiner on the Pritcher Mass tests," Chaz said. "A man named Alexander Waka. He gave me a special test and made it possible for me to be here."

A second went by with no response from her.

"*Chaz?*" she said then. "*Is that right? It doesn't make sense.*"

"It's a fact," he said grimly. "Square that with the fact you say I've got no unusual talents."

"*Oh, Chaz!*" There was another little pause, perhaps half a breath of pause. "*How can I get the point over to you? It's you I'm worried about. I want you to take care of yourself and not let anyone hurt you. You've got to realize how it is. No, you don't have any unusual talents. If I hadn't—if I felt differently about you, I could have used my ability to make you do what I wanted without hardly thinking about it.*"

"Thanks," he said.

"*But you've got to face the truth! Talents are something else. Chaz, I want you to live—and the Citadel would just as soon you didn't—unless you can prove useful to them. That's the only reason they're holding off. You just still might turn out to be useful. But the odds are against you. Can you understand that?*"

"That," he said, deeply, remembering back through the many schools, the different places, the childhood in his aunt's house—even when his uncle had been alive it had been his "aunt's house"—"I can believe. All right, tell me what can help me, since there's nothing special about me."

"*All right,*" she said. "*Chaz, to me you're more special than anyone I've ever known; but we have to face facts. You're talented, but there are more talented men and women, particularly on the Mass. You're bright, but there are brighter people. Everything you've got, other people have, and more. There's just one thing. You're unique. Oh, everybody's unique; but they don't operate on the basis of their uniqueness. They don't really march to the tune of their own distant drummer and stand ready to deal with the whole universe singlehanded if the universe doesn't like it.*"

"I don't know if I understand you," he said.

"No," she said, "*that's because you're on the inside looking out. But it's what makes you dangerous to the Citadel, as far*

*as the Mass is concerned. The Mass is subjective—it can be
used by anyone who can work with it; and you see things
differently from anyone else, plus you've got this terrible drive
to make things go the way you want."*

"Who said I had 'this terrible drive'?"

"*I did. Remember I was the one who sat and listened to you
for four hours that night in the game rooms, when you told
me everything there was that mattered to you—*"

She broke off. Her voice fell silent inside him. The physical
sound of a call buzzer was ringing in his airsuit helmet—the
general call signal. Angrily, he opened the communications
channel to his earphones.

". . . Sant? Chaz Sant!" It was the voice of Lebdell Marti.
"Can you hear me? Are you all right up there?"

"Fine," said Chaz.

"You were told to keep your phones open on the general
channel, but they weren't when Ethrya checked just now.
Are you sure you're all right? You haven't been feeling any
different from normal?"

Chaz grinned wolfishly inside his helmet.

"I had a little touch of dizziness just after Ethrya left," he
said. "But it only lasted a second. Good news. I've made contact with the Mass. I'm ready to go to work on it."

No answer came for a long second from the phone. Then
Marti spoke again.

"You'd better come in now," he said. "Yes, I think you'd
better come down. Don't try to do anything with the Mass;
just come in. Come right to my office, here."

"If you say so," said Chaz. "I'll see you in a few minutes."

He cut off communications on his phones again.

"Eileen . . . ?" he said.

But there was no response. Eileen was once again out of
contact. It did not matter. He was sure now he could reach
her any time he wanted to do so.

He went down into the platform, desuited, and descended
to Marti's office. Waiting for him there was not only Marti and

Ethrya—but Jai. Marti, at least, was in no good humor. He
questioned Chaz several times over about exactly what he
had experienced after Ethrya left him. Chaz, a veteran of
such inquisitions since he had been ten years old, calmly repeated that he had felt a slight dizziness after being left alone
by Ethrya; but that this had cleared up immediately and
afterward he had made contact with the Mass. He was fac-
tual in his description of what it had been like, once contact
had been made; except that he made no mention of his conversation with Eileen.

The interview followed classical lines, according to Chaz's
experience. Having failed to make any dent in Chaz's story,
Marti fell into a temporary silence, drumming his fingers on
his desk top.

"Of course," he said, at last, "we've only got your word for
the fact you made Mass contact. That, in itself, could be a
hallucination like the hallucination you evidently had the
first time you were up there with Jai. Don't you think so, Jai?"

"I suppose," said Jai. The tall man looked, Chaz thought,
somewhat uncomfortable.

"In which case, with two hallucinations in a row, we probably shouldn't let you up on the Mass again for fear you
might hurt yourself permanently—"

"Wait a minute!" said Chaz.

Marti broke off, staring at him.

"You may be Director here," said Chaz, grimly, "but maybe
you'll tell me if it's normal practice to take a man off the Mass
permanently because of a first instance in which you only suspect he hallucinated, and a second instance in which he says
he made contact. What did you do when the other workers
first came down saying they'd made contact? Did you suggest
they'd been hallucinating? Or did you take their word for it?
Should I ask around and find out, in case you've forgotten?"

Marti's face went darkly furious. But before he could answer, Ethrya had stopped him with a small hand on his arm.

"We're only trying to protect you, Chaz," she said. "Isn't that right, Jai?"

"That's right," said Jai. "And Chaz, there are other reasons than hallucinations for barring people from the Mass. The Director has to have authority for the good of all the work being done here. On the other hand . . ." He looked at Marti, appealingly.

Marti had himself back under control.

"All right," he said, dryly. "If you feel that strongly, Chaz, you can have another try at the Mass. But one more instance of suspected hallucination and you're off it permanently."

"Good." Chaz, sensing a psychological victory, got to his feet quickly. "I'm ready to go back up right now."

"No," said Marti, definitely. "We'll want at least to give you a thorough checkup and keep you under medical observation for a few days. You can understand that, I hope. You'd better report to the medical section now." He reached out and punched on the desk phone before him. "I'll let them know you're on your way down."

In actuality, it was eight days, as those in the platform counted them, before Chaz was able to get back up on the Mass. The medical section held on to him for tests and observations for three days, then bucked the matter back up to Marti, with a report they would not let Chaz see.

". . . But I don't see why you should worry very much," said the physician in charge of Chaz's case, unofficially.

Marti, however, decided to take time to consider the report. He considered through a fourth and fifth day of idleness for Chaz. The sixth day found Chaz camping in Marti's outer office, without success. The seventh day, Chaz went to find Jai.

"I came out here to work," Chaz told the tall Assistant Director, bluntly. "I'm able to work. He knows it. I don't care how you put it to him, but say I know I'm getting different handling from anyone else on the Mass who's qualified to work; and if I'm not cleared to go upstairs tomorrow, I'm going to start finding ways to fight for my rights. And take my word for it—I'm good at finding ways to fight when I have to."

"Chaz," protested Jai, softly, "that's the wrong attitude. Leb has to think of the good of the Mass and the people working here as a whole—"

He broke off, looking away from Chaz's eyes, which had remained unmovingly on those of the Assistant Director all the while.

"All right," said Jai, with a sigh. "I'll talk to Leb."

He went off. The morning of the next day he came to Chaz.

"Leb says there's only one way you can prove you made contact with the Mass," Jai said. "That's by doing some work on it that will show up as an obvious addition to it in the perceptions of the other workers. Do that, and you'll have proved your case. But he'll only give you one more shot at it. Leb says you can go up and take that shot right now; or you can take as long as you like to get ready before trying it."

"Or, in other words," said Chaz, "I can sit around until self-doubt starts to creep in. No thanks. I'll go up now. Want to come along with me and take a look at my airsuit before I put it on, to make sure it's all right?"

Jai stared at him.

"Why wouldn't your airsuit be all right?"

"I've got no idea," said Chaz, blandly. "Why don't you have a look at it, anyway?"

Jai stared at him a second longer, then nodded with sudden vigor.

"All right," he said. "I'll do that. In fact, I'll go out on the Mass with you, unless you've got some objection."

"No objection. Here we go."

They went upstairs, where Jai actually did examine Chaz's airsuit carefully before they dressed and went out. They went up a nearby mast and changed to a cable car. In mid-cable, Chaz stopped the car.

"Tell me," he said to Jai. "How do you feel about my being allowd to work on the Mass?"

"How do I feel?" Jai stared at him through the faceplate of his airsuit helmet.

The question hung in both their minds. There was a moment of pause—and Chaz moved into that moment, expanding it by opening his mind to admit the Mass-force.

The Mass-force entered. The dark mountain of hurricanes swirled him up and away, even as he saw time slow down and stop for Jai by comparison. Within himself, Chaz chuckled, reaching into his memory attic. What was it Puck had said in *A Midsummer-Night's Dream?*

"I'll put a girdle round about the earth in forty minutes."

He would put a collar and a leash on the Mass in forty seconds—between his question and Jai's answer—unless he very much mistook the abilities of the force he had learned to ride the last time he was up here. If he was mistaken, of course, the whole thing could backfire. But this was the sort of chance he liked to take.

The Mass swung him up into itself. In a millisecond, he was soaring again, rather than being carried off helplessly. He grinned to himself. The workers on the Mass wanted contact with a different world, did they? Well, perhaps he knew of one world out there he could contact that would surprise them all.

He put into the Mass his memory of the cartoon world with towers leaning at crazy angles, all surfaces covered with a thin sheet of flowing water, on which rode great Snails, and where an alien-like tall Praying Mantis spoke to him. He pointed the Mass in search of such a world—

—And he was there. It was just as he remembered it. Except that the water was ice, now; and the air was bitterly cold. He shivered, watching; but the Snails skated as serenely on the frozen surfaces as they had on the liquid; and the

Mantis, unperturbed by, or apparently indifferent to the cold, gazed calmly down at him.

"So you really look like this?" said Chaz. "And your world looks the way I dreamed it?"

"No. It looks the way you picture it," said the Mantis. "And we look the way you imagine us. I talk with the words you give me. You're our translator."

"Am I?" said Chaz. "Well, I'm going to translate everything about you into the Mass, right now."

"No," said the Mantis.

"No?" Chaz stared up at him.

"You seem to believe that either we'll be of some help to you," said the Mantis, "or that you'll be able to use us to help yourself. Both ideas are incorrect."

"What's correct, then?" he asked.

"That we are real, if different from how you are this moment imagining us," said the Mantis. "More than that, you are required to discover for yourself."

"I see," said Chaz; and abruptly, he thought he did. "You're saying we aren't wanted on or in touch with your world? The doors are closed?"

"All doors are closed to you," said the Mantis. "I only answer you now because of our obligation to answer all who come asking."

"That so?" said Chaz. "Who else on the Mass have you told about that?"

"No one but yourself," said the Mantis. "You were the only one who came looking and found us."

"But I found you back before I came to the Mass," Chaz said. "I dreamed about you first when I was back on Earth with no Mass to help me."

"The Mass is on Earth," said the Mantis.

"The Mass on . . . ?" Chaz's mind whirled suddenly. The words of the Mantis seemed suddenly to open up echoing corridors of possibilities. Abruptly, Chaz stared away down bottomless canyons of linked causes and effects, swooping

off toward a conclusion so improbably distant that for all
its vast importance, it was beyond perception. The winds of
the Mass-force shrieked suddenly in his ears like a chorus of
billions of human voices, crying all at once. And among those
who cried, he heard one in particular . . .

He left the Mantis and the cartoon world with its skating
Snails, and he went toward Earth, into darkness, calling.

"Eileen? Eileen, are you there?"

"*Chaz* . . ."

"Eileen? Eileen, answer me. Where are you, someplace in
the Citadel?"

"No." The answer was slower in coming than usual. "*I'm
out now. They've let me go.*"

"Good!" he said. "You're all right, then. Are you back in
our old condominium? When did you get out—what're you
doing now?"

"*Chaz,*" she said. "*Listen. I've got something to talk to
you about—*"

"Go ahead," he told her.

"*The Citadel told me some things before they let me go.
Most of it isn't important. But there's one thing. You know,
the trips to the Mass are all one-way. You won't be coming
back—*"

"No. But you can qualify yourself for the Mass," he said.
"I've been thinking about that. You've already got the talent;
and I can help you. With the two of us out here—"

"No," she interrupted him. "*You're wrong. I'm not able
to qualify and I wouldn't if I could. That's something I didn't
tell you about those of us who used to call ourselves witches.
The Earth is special to us. We'd never leave her. We'll all die
here, first. So you see, I can't go; and you'll never be coming
back. The Citadel reminded me about that; and I'm glad
they did. Because there's no use you and I both going on
making ourselves unhappy. The sooner I settle back into
the way things used to be with me, the better; and the sooner
you settle down out there and forget me, the better.*"

He stared into darkness, hearing the words but absolutely refusing to believe them.

"Eileen?" he said. "What did they do to you? What is this crazy nonsense you're talking? I've never turned back from anything in my life once I started after it. Do you think I'd turn back from you—of all things?"

"*Chaz, listen to me! You've got a chance there. They told me that much. I mean, more than just a chance to fit in on the Mass. If you can be useful to them, you can be one of the ones who goes on to the new world, when it's found. It's not just their promise—that wouldn't mean anything. But they pointed out to me that if you were worthwhile, they'd need you on the new world. And that's true. Only you have to forget me, just as I'm going to forget you—*"

He could see nothing but the darkness. He could read nothing in her voice. But a furious suspicion was building to a certainty in his mind.

"Eileen!" he snapped at her suddenly. "You're crying, aren't you? Why? Why are you crying? What's wrong? WHERE ARE YOU?"

Stiff with anger, he reached back into the Mass-force for strength, found it, and ripped at the darkness that hid her from him. The obscurity dissolved like dark mist, and he saw her. She was stumbling along a rough, grassy hillside, tears streaking her face. There was a fish-belly-white sky above her and a wind was plucking at her green jumpsuit and whipping her hair about her shoulders. All around her, the land was without buildings or any sign of life, including Tillicum. He thought he could even smell the raw, chill, haze-flavored air.

"You're *outside!*" he exploded at her. "Why didn't you tell me? Was that what they meant by saying they'd turn you loose? Why didn't you say they'd put you out of the sterile areas to die of the rot?"

CHAPTER TEN

SHE STOPPED, lifting her head and looking around her, bewilderedly.

"*Chaz?*" she said, "*Chaz, you aren't here, are you? What do you mean, I'm outside?*"

"I can see you."

"*You can . . . see me?*"

She stared around her. Her face was flushed, and her eyes were unnaturally bright. For a moment, she tried with one hand to capture her flying hair and hold it still against the back of her neck, but failed. Her hand fell limply to her side.

"That's right," he said. "And now I know what they've done to you, do you think I'm going to leave you outside to die? I'll come back there—"

"*Leave me alone!*" she cried. "*Just go away and leave me alone! I don't want you back here. I don't want you at all. I just want you to stay where you are and forget about me*

—is that too much to ask? I don't want you—I don't need you!"

"What about the rot?" he demanded. "If you're outside—"

"I'm not afraid of the rot!" she exploded furiously. *"Didn't I tell you when you first brought that unsterilized piece of stone in that it wouldn't infect me? Witches are immune to the rot!"*

"No one's immune to the rot—"

"Witches are. I was—until you made me love you and I lost my talents. Now, if you'll just go away and leave me alone, I can stop loving you and be able to use my craft again. I'll be all right, then; and that's all I want. Why can't I make you understand that? That's all I want—you to go away and stay away. Go away." She screamed it at him. "GO AWAY!"

The violence of her feelings exploded in his mind, leaving him numb. The darkness flowed back and his vision of her was lost; her voice was silent. He was alone, again, emotionally slashed and stunned.

Like a man slowly waking up, he came back to awareness of the cable car on the Mass. Jai was still sitting opposite him and there was enough reflected light around from the cables and the masts for him to see the other's face within his airsuit helmet. Jai's features were slowly molding themselves into a frown of something like decision, as he stared at Chaz. Plainly, the speed-up Chaz had initiated was still making a difference between his own perceived-time and that of the Assistant Director's; but that did not mean Jai was unaware of what went on. Chaz stared back grimly.

Eileen had cut him off, shut him out. Once again, as it had been always, all through his life, he had been thrown back on his own.

He could try again. He could make use of the Mass to force contact on Eileen. But what was the point? She was right, of course. He had caused her to lose her ability to use her paranormal talent. It did not matter that he had not done it deliberately; or that her loss was psychological, rather than real—the practical results had been the same. Also, he had been responsible for everything that had happened to her since meeting him—including being exiled now to the unsterile areas, to rot and die.

As far as that went, she was right about his situation. He could stay on the Mass and prove himself too valuable for the Citadel people here to do without. It did not matter that the cartoon world of the Snails and the Mantis was closed to them. If he could fit in here—he woke suddenly to a realization of the nonsense he was thinking. He was forgetting something he had told her about himself; that he had never in his life turned back from anything he had set out to pursue. It was a simple truth, with no particular courage or virtue involved. It was just the way he was built—he had no gears for going into reverse, so that he could never back off once he had started out after something, and he could not back off now from Eileen. He had fallen in love with her; and she was one of the things he was going to have, or die trying to get. Eileen, and a cure for the conflict of disgust and pity within him that had driven him to the Mass.

So, there was no choice. His decision was a foregone conclusion, he being built the way he was. Since that was the case, the sooner he rescued Eileen from the outside, the better. He turned his attention back to the cable car and Jai.

A droning noise was coming over the earphones and Jai's lips were slowly moving. The speed-up affecting Chaz was evidently still in effect. He had time.

He went back mentally into the Mass, leaving Jai behind. There must be, he thought, a way of using the Mass-force to move him physically from the cable car to Earth. He had considered the chance of making an actual, physical transfer to the cartoon world, back when he had been talking to the Mantis, before the Mantis told him that all doors were closed. If there had been a way to project himself physically to the cartoon world—and that sort of projection had been behind the idea of the Mass from its beginning—it ought to be much simpler to project himself merely to his own world and Eileen.

He examined the matter. It would be necessary to set up some kind of logic-chain that would lead to the conclusion he wanted. He considered the situation as it now stood, with him above the platform, Eileen on Earth, the Mass— Inspiration sparked.

"Project," he thought, was the wrong word to use. To think of projecting something was to think in terms of the physical universe; and whatever mechanism he would use could not be of the physical universe. In fact, by definition it probably should be at odds with physical reality and physical laws. Suppose, to begin with, he threw out the whole idea of physical movement from place to place.

In that case, perhaps what he wanted to accomplish was not so much a projection of his physical body anywhere as a conviction within himself about where he was. As if, once he had completely convinced himself that his body was on Earth, rather than here, then by the force of the Mass the conviction could become reality. Physically he would then be subject to the convictions of his mind.

All right, movement was out. Distance and time could therefore be discarded.

Position could be ignored.

Of course! The Mass itself was actually independent of position. In one sense, naturally, it was here above the platform. But in the sense of the purpose for which it was being built, it would have to be capable of also *being* on another world light years distant—like the cartoon world. If it could be on the cartoon world, why couldn't it be anywhere?

Of course again, it *was* everywhere. Hadn't the Mantis told him that it was back on Earth? The Mantis might have meant more in saying that than was readily perceivable; but nonetheless, the statement by the Mantis had been that the Pritcher Mass *was* on Earth. If the Pritcher Mass was on Earth . . .

Chaz hunted for an anchor for his logic-chain and found it.

Once again, of course. He had contacted the Mantis, the Snails, and the cartoon world, when he was back on Earth. Therefore the Mass had to be there, as the Mantis said. That anchored the logic chain, then. The Mass, beyond dispute, was on Earth. He was in the Mass—therefore he was also on Earth, in principle, since the Mass had no physical limitations on position. The only discrepancy was a matter of conviction—his belief that the platform was surrounding him, rather than the land and sky of a hillside on Earth. He need only alter that conviction. . . .

He tried. For a moment there was only darkness. Then he saw the hillside, but Eileen was not on it. A heavy wave of urgency and fear broke over him, like surf over a man wading out into water where he can swim. He reached to the Mass-force for strength.

And conviction . . .

Became . . .

Reality. He was there.

He stood on the hillside, strangely insulated in his airsuit. Mechanically, he began to strip it off, and was assailed by the iciness of the wind. It had been late fall when he left Earth, and now winter was clearly on its way; although there was yet no sign of snow—the dirty gray snow that would cover ground and vegetation when the cloud cover always overhead opened up with precipitation.

The chill was too strong. Under the airsuit, he had been wearing only the light coveralls of the summer-temperatured Mass platform. He stopped removing his airsuit and pulled it back on again, all but the helmet which he left lying on the ground. Redressed, he felt more comfortable. The airsuit was not built for warmth, and its gray, rubbery fabric, uninflated, bunched around him as he moved; but it stopped the wind.

He looked around. The blocking-out Eileen was doing to him still held. He could not locate her by any paranormal means. He looked at the ground, but it held no message for him. He had been born and raised in the sterile areas; and even if he had not he doubted he would have been the sort of wilderness expert who could follow a trail left by someone in open country. That left only the ordinary uses of his mind as means to find her.

Eileen, also, would have been born and raised in the sterile areas. Surely she would have been in search of some kind of shelter. Equally as surely, she would have wanted to take advantage of as much protection from the wind as possible while she searched. To the lower side of the downslope at his left and stretching away over further rolling hills to the horizon, the visible ground was clear except for an occasional tree or clump of bushes. To his right, along the crown of the hill, and thickening as it ran ahead, was a belt of fairly good-sized pine and spruce trees. The wind should be less among them. Chaz headed toward the trees in the direction he remembered Eileen had been headed when he had last viewed her.

In spite of the airsuit, in the open he chilled rapidly. However, once he reached the trees the wind was indeed less; and also by that time he had begun to warm himself up with the exercise of walking. He moved just inside the edge of the trees, keeping his eyes open for any sign of more solid shelter.

A mile or so along, he came upon the remnants of a barbed-wire fence running through the edge of the wood. In this country, where family farms had been the rule, a fence usually meant a farmhouse not too far away. A farmhouse could mean shelter of some sort, unless it had been burned down.

Eileen would almost certainly have followed such a fence. But which way? Chaz mulled it over, guessed that she would have been most likely to go the way that was closest to the direction in which she had already been traveling, and went that way himself. The fence continued through the trees, emerged in a small, open swampy area, where it circled a pond and climbed a small hill. On the other side of the hill there was no house, but something almost as good—a somewhat overgrown but still recognizable asphalt road, which to the right led out of sight over yet another hill, but to the left led to something that seemed almost certain to be a clump of buildings, or even a small town. Chaz took the road to the left.

As he got close to what he had seen up the road to the left, the hope of a small town evaporated. What he finally made out was what looked to have been a roadside filling station, store, and garage, with a house and barn sitting closely behind the station. As he got nearer to the clump of buildings, he moved more cautiously. There was no law outside the sterile areas.

He had been traveling in the dry ditch on the right side of the road, instinctively; and the autumn-dried vegetation on either side of him was tall enough to screen him from anyone but an observer concentrating on the ditch with a pair of binoculars. Field grass, coneflower, and tansy were mingled along the side of the ditch away from the road; and frequent stalks of milkweed stood stiff and rustling in the wind, their pods split open and emptied at this late stage of the year. Nonetheless, as he came closer to the buildings, he increased his caution further, crouching down so that he could only see the roofs ahead of him above the tops of the vegetation.

He slowed at last to a stop, less than a hundred yards from the rusted and broken shapes of the gasoline pumps he could see even through the grass and milkweed stems. He was in something of a quandary. If Eileen had taken shelter in the ruins up ahead, then he wanted to get to her as soon as possible. But if there was somebody else instead of her in the buildings, or if others were holding her captive there, the last thing he wanted to do was to walk boldly up to the place in plain sight.

He turned and left the ditch, crawling on his belly into the grass and weeds of the field to his right. He made a swing of about twenty or thirty meters out into the field and then headed once more toward the house and store, with which he estimated he was now level.

The airsuit was clumsy for crawling along the ground; and it was little enough compensation that here, down against the earth, the wind bothered him a great deal less, so that it seemed much warmer. In fact, with the effort of crawling, he was soon sweating heavily. His knees and elbows were protected from scrapes by the tough material of the airsuit, but rocks and stumps poked and bruised him, while little, sharp lengths of broken grass and weeds managed to get in the open neck of his airsuit and down his collar.

He was working up a good, hot anger at these minor tortures, when a sudden realization checked him and he almost laughed out loud. He had paused to rest a second and catch his breath long enough to swear under his breath—when it struck him abruptly that, in the face of all common sense, he was enjoying this. The situation might be both dangerous and miserable; but, except for a few moments on the Mass and after the train wreck, he had never felt so alive in his life. It was something to discover.

Having rested enough, he continued, less concerned with his minor discomforts and more alert to the general situation he was in. And it was a good thing he was so; for even at that he nearly blundered into trouble.

If he had not been crawling along with his nose no more than three hand's breadths above the ground, he would never have noticed the thin, dark transverse line that appeared among the weeds just ahead. As it was he saw it without recognizing what it was until he had crawled within inches of it. His first thought was that it was simply a long, thin grass stem fallen on its side. But this theory evaporated as he got closer. Still, it was not until he was up against it that he recognized it for what it actually was—a thin, taut wire stretching across the field just below the tops of the weeds.

Had he been walking he would not have seen it until he tripped over it; he had no reason to look for any such thing

in the first place. As it was, encountering it slowly, he had a
chance to think about what it might mean; and the friendly
old cluttered attic of his memory helped him out with bits
and pieces of information read in the past. The wire could
only be there to stop intruders like himself; and it might connect with anything from a warning system to a nearby cache
of explosive.

He lay still thinking about it. If nothing else, the wire was
evidence that there was someone already holed up in the
buildings ahead; and if that was so, then Eileen, if she was
there at all, was almost undoubtedly a prisoner. Charity
would not be likely among sick and dying people in this de-
cayed, inhospitable land. But if there were unfriendly people
in the buildings—possibly even now keeping a watch—Chaz
would have his work cut out for him to get to the buildings
without being seen.

He lifted his head among the weeds to squint at the sky
overhead. As always, the sun was invisible behind the sullen
haze and cloud bank; but from the light he judged that the
early winter afternoon was not more than an hour or two
from darkness. When the dark came, it would come
quickly. There were no lingering sunsets, nowadays—nor any
moon or stars visible as guides, once the night had come.

Just at this moment he stiffened where he lay, like a hunted
animal hearing the sounds of its hunters. A voice cried from
somewhere far behind him, in the opposite direction from
the house. The words it called were recognizable, half
chanted, on a high, jeering note:

"Rover! Red Rover! Red Rover, come over. . . ."

The voice died away and there was silence. He waited; but
it did not call again. He looked at the wire once more, and
estimated that he could wriggle under it. It had evidently
been set high so as to clear all the humps and rises of the
ground along its route. He rolled over on his back and began
to wriggle forward again.

Once past the wire, he turned belly-down again and con-

tinued on at as good speed as he could make without thrash-
ing around in the weeds and perhaps drawing attention. He
thought that he should not be too far from the relatively
open area that had once been a yard surrounding the buildings; and in fact, shortly, he came up against the rotting
stumps of what had once been a wooden fence. He passed
this and the ground underneath was more even and less lit-
tered with stones. Also, here the weeds were not as thickly
clustered.

He was racing now, however, against the end of the daylight, which could not be much more than half an hour off.
So far he had encountered no more wires; but the thought
that someone might possibly be watching him from the buildings sent a crawling feeling down his spine. He paused and
peered ahead through the now-thin screen of grass and weeds.

He saw the side of the house, wooden shakes weathered
and stained to a near-earth shade. What looked like three
grave mounds, two with crosses half fallen down, were in the
yard to his right. Above him a couple of broken windows, one
above the other, faced in his direction; but there was no sign
of anyone peering out of them. To his right was a door, above
some broken steps. The door sagged on its hinges and stood
slightly ajar inward—in spite of a cleaner, newer piece of
board that had been nailed diagonally across its vertical cracks
to hold them together. That new board shouted of danger;
but the door ajar was an invitation, with night coming on.

Chaz wormed his way to the wall of the house, and then
crawled along the foot of the wall until he came to the door.
Slowly, carefully, he lifted his head until he could see around
the frame and into the gap where the door hung open.

It took a long moment for his eyes to adjust to the inner
shadow; but when they did, he saw nothing but a small,
empty room, and a doorway beyond leading into a further
room that seemed to have a window, or some other source
of light; for it was quite bright by comparison with the first
room.

Chaz dumped caution and hesitation together and squirmed his way over the threshold into the building. Once inside, he scrambled to his feet quickly and stood listening. But he heard nothing. A faint unpleasant smell he could not identify troubled him.

Looking around, he saw a heavy bar leaning against the wall beside the door; and iron spikes driven into the frame and bent up as supports. He reached out for the door and pushed it slightly closed; but it did not creak—surprisingly, it did not creak. He pushed it all the way shut and put the bar in place. Turning, he went further into the building.

Plainly, it had been a large farm-type home once upon a time, but its rooms were empty now, except for spider webs, dust, and rubble. He went all through the rooms on the ground floor before realizing that the smell that bothered him was coming from upstairs.

Cautiously, he took the broad but broken stairs, lit by a paneless window on the landing above them. As he went up the smell grew rapidly stronger. He followed it to its source in a room on the floor above; and found what he was after.

He stepped into a room that had a piece of transparent plastic—non-refractive, as glass would not have been—stretched across its single, tall window. A small iron stove—unlit—stood in one corner, with a stovepipe going through the wall behind it. In the room were sacks and boxes, tools and two old-fashioned rifles, a battered overstuffed chair, and a wide bed. On the bed lay Eileen; and on the floor near the door, as if he had dragged himself, or had been dragged, that far before the effort gave out, was what was left of a man. It was the source of the smell that had caught Chaz's attention. Up here the stench was sickeningly strong.

Almost choking, Chaz got a grip on the collar of the heavy plastic jacket the dead man was wearing and hauled the whole thing out of the room, down the stairs, and to the door by which he had entered. He unbarred the door, rolled it out, then closed and barred the door again. He went back up the stairs, two at a time, to Eileen.

She was lying on her back on the bed, still in her jumpsuit. Chaz fanned the door to the room back and forth hastily to drive a little fresh air inside, and then went to her. She was half covered by a very old, but surprisingly clean, blanket. As he watched, however, she muttered something and threw it off. Her eyes were half open, her cheeks were pink, and she licked her lips as if she was very thirsty.

". . . The park," she murmured. "You promised, Mommy. The park's open today . . ."

"Eileen," he said, touching the back of his fingers gently to her forehead. "Eileen, it's me. Chaz."

The skin of her forehead burned against his fingers. She flinched away from his touch.

"You promised . . ." she said, "we could go to the park. You promised . . ."

He reached down and unsealed the collar of her jumpsuit. In the late daylight filtering through the transparent plastic on the window, he could just make out small reddish areas on the slim column of her neck. Not ulcers, yet, but inflamed patches. That, and the terribly high fever—the first signs of sickening with the rot.

She must have been outside the sterile areas four or five days already, and caught the rot spores immediately when she was put out, to show signs this far advanced.

"You promised . . ." she said, rolling her head on the bed from side to side. "Mommy, you promised me . . ."

CHAPTER ELEVEN

HIS FIRST THOUGHT was to get her some water. Looking around the dim room he caught sight of a five-gallon milk can not far from the stove. He went to it and lifted it. It was heavy and sloshed with contained liquid. He worked off the tight, heavy cover and saw a colorless liquid within.

Cautiously, he tasted it. It was certainly water—how clean and how pure, there was no way of telling. But, on the other hand, this was no situation in which he could pick and choose. A small aluminum pan with a bent handle hung from a nail in the wall nearby. He half filled the pan with water and, taking it back to the bed, managed to lift Eileen's head and get her to drink. When she realized there was water at her lips, she drank thirstily, but without coming out of the delirium of her fever.

He took the empty pan back to its nail and set about examining the room they were in. The removal of the dead body and the door he had left open to the room had improved the

air considerably; but the coolness of the place was now beginning to be noticeable to him. It could be as frigid in this
house as it would be outside, before dawn.

A distant, crying voice halted him like the sudden pressure
of a gun muzzle against his ribs.

"Rover. Oh, Rover . . . Red Rover . . ."

The cry came from outside somewhere. But, if his ears
were right, not from the same quarter of the open fields as the
earlier voice, which had sounded behind him. A moment
later, his hearing was vindicated, as the voice he had first
heard called again, this time plainly from the same direction
he had heard it before.

"Rover. Red Rover . . ."

It had barely finished before two other voices sounded,
each from directions from which he had not yet heard. He
stepped quickly to the window and looked out.

He saw nothing. He squinted against the feeble glare of the
red-stained clouds behind which the sun must be almost on
the horizon; but he still saw nothing. Looking back into the
room, he let his eyes adjust and glanced around. If the dead
man he had just gotten rid of had been holed up here, he
might have had some means of observation—

He found what he was looking for; a pair of heavy binoculars hung by their strap almost beside the window. He had
stared right at them earlier, without recognizing the purpose
in their position. He reached them now and held them to his
eyes.

They were powerful—possibly even 7x10—and for a long
moment as the light faded, he could not hold them steady
enough to sweep the hilltop area a few hundred meters away
at which he was looking. Then, he got one elbow braced
against the window frame on one side and began to look
along the hilltop.

He saw nothing and was just about to put the glasses away
when a figure rose to its feet as casually as if it was on a street
back in one of the sterile areas. Chaz had already lowered the

binoculars and he saw the figure without their aid. He jerked
the binoculars back to his eyes and hunted jerkily for the
shape he had just seen, sweeping past it twice before he could
hold it steadily in his field of amplified vision.

It was of a man in the lower half of a jumpsuit and a bulky
red sweater. In the binoculars, he seemed to leap forward at
Chaz—it was like looking at him from an actual distance of
less than a dozen meters. Chaz blinked, for he had seen the
face he was looking at before. It was the face of the man he
had seen sprawled, apparently dead, beside the wrecked railway motor cart and spilled cartons.

Chaz continued to stare at the face he recognized. This
man was not dead—in fact, he was looking damned healthy
considering the ulcer spots Chaz had seen on his neck before
the train wreck and which were still there, now. As Chaz
looked, the man cupped his hands on either side of his mouth
and shouted in the direction of the buildings.

"Rov—er! Red Rover! Red Rover, come over . . ."

The cry seemed to linger under the darkening sky and the
red-streaked clouds behind the man. Then he took one quick
step backward, as if he stepped down below the brow of the
hill, and disappeared.

As if his going had been a signal, the red streaks began to
fade, the little glare dwindled from the clouds, and the light
began to fade with a rapidity that woke Chaz suddenly to an
awareness of his situation.

He hung the binoculars hastily on their nail and turned.
Somewhere in here, there must be some means of making a
light. He looked instinctively toward the stove and saw nothing useful there. He looked about the room, and actually
looked past, before he had the sense to bring his eye back to
it, an antique oil lamp, standing on a table in the room. Its
appearance was a cross between that of a gravy boat and a
pointed-toe slipper, badly modeled in cheap crockery.

It was, in fact, an imitation of an ancient lamp from the
Mediterranean area. He had seen the same sort of thing ad-

vertised as an aid to meditation. He pounced on it, found
it half filled with liquid and with a rag of porous towel-
plastic stuck in its spout end for a wick. There was a quite
modern fusion incense lighter on the table beside the lamp;
and a second later he had the wick lit. A wavery illumination
from the bare flame lit up the room.

He spun around to the window, cursing himself. Their
lighted room would stand out like a beacon. There was a roll
of cloth above the window; a curtain, hung on nails. He
stepped to it now and unrolled a blackout shade consisting
of several layers of dark cloth backed by a sheet of opaque,
gray plastic.

He arranged it over the window and turned back to do a
thorough job of exploring the room. As he moved slowly
about it, checking everything he found, he was astonished at
how much in the way of useful equipment was contained
within its four walls. Much of it was makeshift, like the old-
fashioned milk can that held their water supply. But much
of it also showed the result of ingenuity and work—a great
deal of work for a man who could hardly have survived the
rot for more than a couple of months while he was setting
up this place.

There was food, fuel, weapons, ammunition, spare clothing, soap, a few medicines ranging from aspirin to capsules of
a general anti-viral agent—even, tucked in one corner, a box of
what seemed to be home-brew beer. Having completed his
survey, Chaz turned to the most immediately important matter of getting some heat into the room. It was possibly his
imagination, but the temperature seemed to be dropping very
fast.

He covered Eileen with the available bedclothes, and this
time she did not throw them off, though her head was still
very hot. He gave her another drink of water and turned to
the stove. There was paper, kindling, and wood chunks piled
beside it. Using the incense lighter, he got a fire going; and
much faster than he would have expected, the stove was
throwing out heat.

He went to the window and pulled the edge of the black-out curtain aside a fraction. Outside the permanently clouded night was full-fallen; and the darkness was as complete as that mind-darkness he had encountered on the Mass when he had tried to make verbal contact with Eileen. The similarity triggered an inspiration in him. What was the use of having achieved his partnership with a psychic force like the Mass, if he did not put it to use? Maybe the Mass could help Eileen.

How?

The immediate question that popped into his mind was like a brick wall suddenly thrown up in his way. He replaced the blackout curtain and stood by the window, looking across at Eileen under the covers of the bed and thinking. Wild possibilities chased themselves through his head. Maybe the Mass could be used to transport Eileen back in time to a point where she had not yet inhaled any of the rot spores— to a time when she was still safely inside the protection of the domes and airlocks of the sterile areas. Maybe the Mass could alter the facts of the situation so that she had never been infected with spores at all. Maybe . . .

His thoughts lit up with a new enthusiasm. Maybe the Mass could be used to remove the spores already in her lungs —to rid her body completely of all physical elements of the rot? Certainly the Mass was able to transport physical objects like his body from the Mass back to here . . . his enthusiasm faded. Considered coldly, even this began to look like a wild hope.

However, it would not hurt to tie the Mass in both to Eileen and himself under the general command to aid and assist them. He reached out with his mind for contact with the massive psychic construct, willing himself to imagine it and his connection with it as he had experienced it and pictured it back above the platform. . . .

. . . And touched nothing.

The same wall of blackness he had not been able to push aside when he had last tried to contact Eileen verbally now barred him from the Mass itself. He struggled to get through the barrier but it was no use. In her delirium, Eileen was still blocking her immediate area from the platform and the Mass, where she thought he still was.

He gave up and returned his attention to the room, looking across it to where she lay in the bed. She was apparently asleep, if restive with fever; but evidently sleep and sickness together did not interfere with unconscious use of her paranormal talents. Until her fever went down enough for her to recognize him, there was no hope of his reaching her to inform her of the changed situation.

Well, he told himself, there was no use getting worked up about it. On the bed, now, Eileen stirred restlessly and licked her lips again. He took her another drink and lifted her head while she drank thirstily.

"Eileen?" he said. "It's me—Chaz. Chaz."

But her eyes stared past him. Gently, he laid her head back on the pillow; and she shifted it immediately away from the spot where he laid it down, as if the pillow bothered her. He reached to plump it up for her and felt something hard beneath it.

He lifted one end of the pillow, caught a glimpse of something dark, and drew it out. It was a thick, black notebook with a sheaf of folded papers, larger than the pages in the notebook, pushed between its front cover and the pages.

He took it over to the table where the oil lamp burned stinkingly and pulled up the chair. Seating himself, he opened the book and took out the sheaf of papers. They were folded lengthwise, in a bunch. He unfolded them. The writing at the top of the first sheet was printed in large letters—

LAST WILL AND TESTAMENT—Harvey Olkin

He looked down at what was written below.

"I, Harvey Olkin, being of sound mind and body except for dying of the rot, hereby bequeath this place and everything in it

to whoever finds it after I'm gone; just as it was bequeathed to me by the man who was here before I was. And the only thing I ask of whoever takes my place, is that he or she buries me down in the yard, like I buried the man before me and he buried the man before him, and so on. It's not much to ask, considering what you're getting and how it's been passed on down by four people already. We're giving you the chance to die comfortable, which almost nobody shoved outside gets; and all any of us ever asked is that you take good care of the stuff while you still can, and finish the job by burying whoever took care of it before you—in this case, me.

The whole story is in the diary, which you ought to keep up, like the rest of us did. If you play fair, maybe the next one will bury you, too, when the time comes. Maybe you don't want to think about that just yet; but take it from me, when the breathing begins to get hard toward the end, you take a lot of comfort out of knowing you'll be put down in the earth right, the way people ought. Anyway, that's how it is. The other papers under this one will give you what you need to know to run things and keep the Rovers and scavengers away; and the rest of the story's in the diary. This is about as much as I've got strength to write now.

Harvey Olkin

In fact, the handwriting had become more and more illegible toward the end of the message and the signature was a scrawl. Chaz would not have been able to decipher it at all if Harvey Olkin had not written his name more plainly at the beginning of the will.

Chaz checked through the rest of the loose papers. They were sketches, descriptions, and lists dealing with the house, its supplies and defenses, in careful detail. Plainly, each new owner of the house had added to its strength and comforts in various ways. Chaz put the loose papers aside and began to read through the diary. It commenced with entries by the first man to hole up in the house, a nephew of the family that had owned it before the coming of the rot; a man who had

deliberately sought this place out when he was exiled from
the sterile areas for some unmentioned civil crime.

It was two hours before Chaz reached the blank pages in
the book where the record ended. When it was done, he sat
in the light of the guttering, already several-times-refilled oil
lamp, feeling closer to these four dead men than he had to
anyone in his life, with the exception of Eileen. There was
something right here—something that chimed in with his
own feelings—about the way these four had spent their last
days under the shadow of a certain death. Just as there was
something wrong about a whole race of people bottling themselves up in small enclaves of sterile environment and waiting passively for an inevitable end. He could not believe that
they would be so accepting and passive in the face of death.
Something, his instincts said, was wrong about such a reaction. It was the same sort of wrongness that had driven him
to try for work on the Mass rather than yield to a similar de-
featism. If only he could find some evidence of others troubled by, or rejecting of, the idea that their doom was over-
whelming, he had thought once. Well, here were four others
who had at least done something while dying.

Perhaps, though, he thought, that was the trouble even
with these four. Even they had not rejected death as fully as
they should. They had not rejected it quite enough.

He chewed his lower lip. Somehow, there must be a logic-
chain that would fit it all together to his satisfaction. All of it
—the rot, the sterile areas, the Mass, these four. . . . But the
connections he sought seemed to slip away from him just as
his mind grasped them. Perhaps the puzzle was not complete.
There could be parts missing. . . .

He gave up, wrapped himself in a blanket, settled himself
in his chair, and slept.

When morning came, Eileen was still delirious with fever
and continued not to recognize him. In between moments of
caring for her, he investigated the place they were in, the loose

sheets of paper from the diary in his hand. What he found amazed him all over again.

To begin with, all four buildings in the group—the store up in front of the house, the barn, a sort of garage-like building beside the house toward its back, and the house itself— were connected by tunnels. Each one had an observation point near the peak of its roof, from which he could get a quick view of the surrounding area. The garage-like building held the remains of two ancient cars and a remarkable array of metal and woodworking tools. In the basement of the house itself, the power pump unit with its dead fusion pack had been disconnected from a wellhead, and a hand pump fitted on to the pipe to bring up water. Extra supplies of firewood and a veritable mountain of canned goods were stored in the same basement.

Chaz discovered that once he had covered some five meters of distance in the open from the back door of the house, he was in an area where the house, the barn, and the garage structure shielded him on all sides. It was here the three previous graves had been dug; and it was here that, on that same afternoon, Chaz fulfilled his duty of burying the body of Harvey Olkin.

He took one of the rifles along with him on the task. He had never fired one; but the drawings and instructions on the loose sheets of paper were explicit. When he was done, he took the rifle back upstairs to the room where Eileen was and left it there, leaning against the wall, while he searched the fields about them with the binoculars, from windows on all four sides of the house.

He saw nothing; and he was just putting the binoculars away, back on their nail beside the plastic-covered window, when a movement out in the field caught his eye. He dropped the glasses, snatched up the rifle, pointed it, and pulled the trigger—all without thinking.

There was a shell in the chamber of the weapon; but the hammer merely clicked harmlessly on it. A dud. The diary

had warned that the ammunition for the guns was getting
old and unreliable.

A little sheepishly, Chaz lowered the rifle. If it had gone
off, he would have fired through the plastic sheeting doing
service as a windowpane. A waste of good material. The mo-
mentary check had given him time to think. The movement
he had seen was still a good fifty yards from the house. Anyone crawling through the weeds at that distance was in no
danger of rushing them suddenly.

Chaz put the gun down again and once more picked up the
binoculars. He had to wait until he saw the weed tops sway
unnaturally before he could locate what had caught his eye
in the first place. But when they did, he was able to focus the
glasses in on it and the figure of a man in a red sweater and
the lower half of a jumpsuit became easily visible, crawling
toward the house, dragging something long and metallic-
looking with him.

Carefully keeping his attention on the spot, Chaz put
down the binoculars, loosened and folded back a corner of
the plastic window covering, and took aim with the rifle
through the opening. Now that he knew where the man was,
he could make him out fairly easily, even with the naked eye.
He lined up the sights on the back of the red sweater . . . then
found he could not do it.

It might be one thing to shoot the man if he was coming
up the stairs at them, but to put a bullet in him while he was
still just crawling through the field in their direction was
something Chaz was not yet up to doing. Carefully, Chaz
aimed well wide of the crawling figure and pulled the trigger.
The rifle clicked. Another bad round. The third time Chaz
tried, however, sound exploded in the room and the gun wal-
loped his shoulder. He saw a puff of dust out in the grass a
good five meters to the left of the figure.

The next thing that happened was unexpected.

There was a sharp crack above his head, and a smell of
burning. Chaz looked up, startled, to see a smoldering hole in

the wall above the window and another blackish hole in the plaster of the room's ceiling. Chaz felt cold. He knew next to nothing about firearms, but he knew more than a little—even if the knowledge was essentially theoretical—about laser guns.

"All right in there!" a voice cried from the field. "Now you know. I can play rough, too—but I don't want to. I just want to talk to you. All right? I'm willing to come in if you're willing to come out!"

Chaz stood, thinking.

"How about it?" called the voice from outside.

"Hang on to your teeth, Red Rover!" Chaz shouted back. "I'll tell you in a minute."

"I'll come into the yard, no weapons. You come out of the back door, no weapons. I just want to talk. Make up your mind, in there."

Chaz came to a decision. Snatching up the rifle he had used before and an extra handful of shells, he ran out of the room, downstairs to the basement, and through the tunnel that connected with the garage. The garage had a service door opening inward on the yard, screened by barn and house from the fields around. He opened the door softly, reached out and leaned the rifle against the side of the building, then ran back through the tunnel and upstairs once more to the room where Eileen lay.

"What about it?" the voice was calling from outside. "I'm not going to wait all day."

Chaz struggled to get his breath back, leaning against the wall. After a moment, he managed to call an answer.

"All right. Be right down. I'll step out the back door. You stand up at the edge of the yard. Suit you?"

"Suits me!" the answer floated back.

Chaz turned and went out again and down the stairs toward the same back door by which he had entered the house the day before. He went slowly, making sure he got his breath all the way back before he reached the door. When he did, he opened it cautiously. There was no one in sight. The weeds hid the other man, if indeed he was where he had promised to be.

"You there?" called Chaz through the door.

"I'm here!" The answer came from approximately where it should in the weed tangle.

"I'm going to count to three," Chaz called. "When I say 'three,' I'll step out of the door and you stand up. All right?"

"Hell, yes!" the answer was almost contemptuous. "I keep telling you I only want to talk. If I wanted something else, I could burn that place down around your ears before dark."

"Don't try it!" said Chaz. "One . . . two . . . three!"

With the last word, he stepped out on the back step. The man he had expected to see, the man he had viewed in the binoculars and seen apparently dead at the train wreck, stood up at the edge of the yard. He did not wait for Chaz to speak or move, but calmly started walking forward, empty-handed.

Chaz broke and ran, at a slant toward the garage building. In ten long strides, the garage itself cut him off from the sight of the advancing man. Chaz snatched up the rifle and turned around with it aimed.

"Take it easy," he heard the voice of Red Rover saying as he approached the corner of the garage. "I told you talk, and I meant talk—"

He stepped into view around the corner of the house, saw Chaz with the rifle, and stopped abruptly, but without obvious alarm. Whatever else might be true of him, he had courage.

"That's pretty dirty pool you play," he said. He waggled the hands at his sides. "I said I'd come unarmed, and I did."

"And there's no dirty pool in bringing a whole gang against this one place?" Chaz answered, still keeping the rifle on him. "I don't know about you. I'm out to stay alive."

"Who says I want you dead?" Red Rover's eyes flickered over toward the graves, and his face grew shrewd, as he stared at the one Chaz had dug so recently. "Girl die?"

"What girl?" demanded Chaz.

"You know what girl. She's the one I wanted to speak to you about. If she's dead already, that's an end to it."

"I don't know what you're talking about," said Chaz.

"You're a headache," Red Rover said. "You can't seem to get it through your skull I'm not against you. Hell, I've been keeping the Rover packs off your back for two years now. You didn't think you were doing it all alone, did you?"

He stared at Chaz challengingly.

"Go ahead," Chaz said. "You're doing all the talking."

"That's all there is to it. If the girl's dead, there's no problem. If not, I have to stay next to her until she is. The only thing is, I have to know for sure that she's dead. If it's her you've got buried there"—he nodded at the recent grave—"you're going to have to dig her up so I can see her."

On the verge of telling him in plain Anglo-Saxon what he could do with himself, Chaz checked. There was some kind of mystery involved in all this; and he was more likely to get answers if he sounded halfway agreeable.

"No," he said, briefly.

Red Rover gazed shrewdly at him once more.

"Who was she?" Rover asked. "Some relative? She had to know the place was here. They put her out of a Gary, Indiana, airlock; and she came straight here. Over sixty klicks—forty-three miles according to the old road system, only she went straight across country. Sorry about that; but I've got to see her dead, if you want to be left alone."

Chaz made a decision. After all, he still had the rifle and Red Rover was unarmed.

"She's not dead," he answered. "I'll show her to you." He gestured with the rifle barrel at the back door of the house. "In that way."

Rover turned and headed for the door. Chaz followed, carrying the rifle along his right leg and side, shielded from whoever might be in the fields watching. They went through the house and upstairs to where Eileen still lay in her fever. Red Rover looked dispassionately down at her, stepped to the

side of the bed and peeled back one of her eyelids, then examined the inflamed spots on her neck and upper chest area.

"She's on her way," he said, stepping back from the bed
and looking at Chaz. "Maybe she's got four months yet,
maybe only ten days more. But she's caught it. Lucky the
worst is over—except for the choking at the end. She'll be
coming out of that fever any time now. But I suppose you
know that as well as I do. She's as good as dead."

"No," said Chaz. "She won't die."

He had not expected to speak with such intensity; and the
deep, harsh tone of his voice startled even him. Apparently
it startled Red Rover even more, however, for the other man
shied like a startled horse, taking half a step back from Chaz.

"What do you mean?" Rover snapped. "You don't mean
she's another? You don't mean it runs in families?"

"Families? What runs in families?" Chaz demanded.

"What do you think I'm talking about?" retorted Red
Rover. "The same thing you and I've got in common. The
reason I've helped keep the scavengers off your back these
last two years—though you don't seem to have appreciated it
much. Don't you realize we've got to stick together, us immunes?"

CHAPTER TWELVE

CHAZ DREW a deep breath.

"So that's it," he said. "You're immune to the rot."

"Didn't I say so? Just like you—" Red Rover broke off. "Wait a minute, friend. You *have* been living here the last two years, haven't you?"

His face changed, swiftly. Just as swiftly, Chaz brought up the muzzle of the rifle, which had sagged floorward during the conversation.

"Easy. I'm immune. So's she," said Chaz. "But no, I haven't lived here for two years. You've got a lot to learn, Red Rover. But so have I. Let's talk it over like sensible people. I'll give you my promise we're on the same side."

"Are we?" Rover's face was still tight. He looked over at Eileen. "How come she's sick then, come to think of it? I never did get sick." His hand went to the ulcer-appearing spots on his throat. "I got so I painted these on in self-protection."

He looked back at Chaz.

"She's sick because she thinks she ought to be," Chaz said.

"Ought to be?" Red Rover stared. "How do you know that?"

"Because that's the way the logic-chain runs," said Chaz. The other's features kept their expression. "Don't you know about Heisenbergian chain-perception—the Pritcher Mass?"

"Sure, I've heard"—Red Rover's face relaxed—"all about that parapsychological crazy-business. You're not trying to tell me there's something to it?"

"Of course," said Chaz. "Why shouldn't there be?"

"Why," said Rover, "because it's just another one of those government boondoggles. They're all alike. A bunch of politicians have to justify their jobs; so they dream up something to spend the product of the working citizen. The thing they dream up is always some of that rarefied junk that never had a chance of working; but it keeps peoples' minds occupied for a few years until they have to scrap it and dream up something new."

Chaz stared at the other man. It was hard to believe that the ignorance Red Rover was professing could be honest. On the other hand, if it actually was honest— Chaz felt a silent explosion of understanding in his mind. If it was honest, it could lead to an explanation of why this man had survived while the four who had occupied this house had died of the rot.

". . . But you're trying to tell me it works?" Rover was saying.

"Look," Chaz said. "Take the chair, there. I'll sit down on the side of the bed, and we'll start from the beginning."

They sat down.

"All right," said Chaz. "Werner Heisenberg was a physicist. He stated you could know either the position or the velocity of a particle exactly, but not both exactly, at the same time."

"Why not?"

"Wait please," said Chaz. "I'm no physicist myself. Let's not get tangled up in explanations right at the start. Heisenberg produced this Principle of Uncertainty. From that, sometime in the 1960s, came the notion that alternate universes might actually exist.

"Alternate whats?"

"I flip a coin or a token," Chaz said. "It lands tails. I win a bet from you because of that. Things go on to happen as a result of that bet. That's one universe of possible results. But what if it landed heads? Then you'd win. Different things would go on to happen from *that*. That'd be another possible universe."

"I don't—"

"Never mind," said Chaz. "Just go on listening. Suppose everytime there was an either-or, two-way choice, the universe split into two universes, with one chain of things happening as a result to make things one way, say from the coin coming up heads, and one to make them another, from it coming up tails. Each chain would be a chain of logical results—what we call a logic-chain. Do you follow me there?"

"No," said Red Rover.

"Do you know the poem," Chaz asked, "that goes—'*For want of a nail, a horseshoe was lost/ For want of a horseshoe, a horse was lost—*'?"

"Sure—'*For want of a horse a rider was lost.*

" '*For want of a rider a message was lost,*

" '*For want of a message a battle was lost.*

" '*And all for the want of a horseshoe nail!*'—I see," said Red Rover. "In one universe they lose a nail and pretty soon they lose a kingdom. In the other, they have the nail and they get to keep the same kingdom. So that's a logic-chain, is it?"

"Right," said Chaz. "Now, since there're two-way choices like that happening all the time, somebody who could look ahead and see which way each split-off chain might go on each choice he made could pick and choose just the right choices he needed to get him the final result he wanted. Follow?"

"Go on," said Red Rover.

"Right, then. Now, this world of ours is sick and getting sicker. Regular physical sciences are up against impossibilities in the way of time and distance, in finding a new world for people to escape to so they can survive. But non-physical science can maybe ignore those impossibilities, to build us something to find a world and get us there. So suppose we decide to use chain-perception to build the non-physical help we need. We start with knowing what we want—a something to get a clean, fresh world for us—and with that end in mind, we start picking and choosing, first among immediate either-or choices; then among the choices that result from that picking and choosing. And so on. A man named James Pritcher sat down to do that as just an academic exercise, fifteen years ago; and what he came up with was that somewhere out beyond Pluto we needed to begin trying to create a non-physical device, a psychic machine that we could use to find a way to the sort of world we wanted and a way to get us all to it."

He paused to draw a breath.

"And that's it," he wound up. "That's what the Pritcher Mass is, a psychic machine; and it's already mostly built. I just came from there. I can use chain-perception. That's why I tell you I'm not going to catch the rot; and Eileen's just suffering from an imaginary case of it."

There was a long silence after he finished. Red Rover stared back at him for a while, then looked at Eileen, then back to him.

"So," Rover said, "her name's Eileen, is it? They never did tell me her name."

"Who's they?" Chaz demanded.

"The Citadel people." Red Rover stood up and Chaz snatched for the rifle. "Put it down. You're right. We've got a lot to talk about; but I'm going to have to go back outside now and do a little talking on my own, or you'll have all fourteen of my Rovers on your neck to rescue me from you."

He looked around the room.

"You've got some way of making a light at night here, haven't you?" he asked.

Chaz nodded.

"All right then; I'll come back just at dark and we can talk at night when none of them know I'm spending time with you. Leave that door downstairs open for me about sunset."

He went out; and Chaz heard his boots clattering down the stairs. For a while after the sound of them had ceased, Chaz continued to sit where he was, thinking. Eileen was immune to the rot because she was a witch—that is, because she had paranormal abilities. If he himself was immune to the rot, as the logic-chains he considered seemed to show, he could swear it was because he had proved to himself he also had paranormal abilities. But here was Rover, who was also immune, and didn't even believe in paranormal abilities, let alone having any—or did he?

It would be interesting, thought Chaz, to find out.

Still later that afternoon, as Chaz was busily marking x's, o's, and squares, with a graphite lubricating pencil from the garage, on one side of a stack of small pieces of paper he had made by tearing up a blank sheet from the diary, he heard his name called.

"Chaz? . . . Chaz?"

It was a very weak voice calling, but it was Eileen's voice. He got up hastily and went over to the bed. She looked up at him with eyes that recognized him; and when he put his hand on her forehead, the forehead was cool and damp.

"What are you doing here, Chaz?" The words were barely more than whispered. Her eyes roamed around the stained plaster of the ceiling above her. "Where are we?"

"Outside," he told her, sitting down on the edge of the bed beside her.

"Outside? I thought perhaps I was back in the Citadel, somewhere, and they'd brought you back too— Chaz! When did you get back from the Mass?"

"Yesterday," he said. "Don't worry about that now."

"But you said we were outside!" She tried to lift her head, but he pushed her gently back down again. "I remember now, they put me out. I remember . . . I caught the rot. Chaz—now you'll catch it."

"Easy," he told her. "I'm not going to catch anything. And as for you, you aren't either—and you haven't."

"But I remember. The fever that starts it . . ."

"Just about anybody," said Chaz, "can whip up a pretty good fever if they're thoroughly convinced they ought to be having one. Hospitals in the old days used to be full of people running unexplained fevers. Feel your throat."

She reached up slowly with one hand and ran her fingers over the surface of her neck.

"There aren't any ulcers," she said, wonderingly. "But I had sore spots . . ."

"Not only sore," Chaz said, "they were inflamed, too. But you couldn't quite push them over the edge into real ulcers."

"Why"—her voice was still weak, but it was beginning to be indignant—"do you keep talking like that? Do you think I wanted to catch the rot?"

"No, but you thought you would, anyway; because you'd lost your witch immunity."

She stared at him with eyes that seemed half again as large as usual in the aftermath of her sickness.

"I hadn't?"

"Think about it," he said. "Just lie there and take your time. Think about it."

She lay still. After a second she pushed a hand in his direction. He took it and held it; then looked down at it in a mild sort of surprise at himself for understanding so immediately that that was what she wanted. They sat for a little while. It had been chilly again; and with Red Rover already having visited here, secrecy seemed pointless. So he was running a fire in the stove to warm the room. Only the soft noises as the burning wood fell apart broke the silence around them until Eileen spoke again.

"It *was* a psychological block," she said, "my thinking I'd lost my paranormal talents because I'd fallen in love the way a witch isn't supposed to do. I knew it was just a block; but I couldn't seem to do anything about it. But now they put me outside; and in spite of the block, the witch immunity saves me. It doesn't make sense."

"Sure it does," he said. "I've had the chance lately to make sense out of a lot of things. The instinct to survive is back in the old, primitive machinery of your brain, away behind all that fancy modern wiring that has to do with conscious belief and psychological blocks. What the survival instinct said when you landed outside was—'To hell with what's haywire up front. We'll deal with the rot the way we know how; keep her alive and let her figure it all out afterward.'"

She did not answer him for a moment. Then she spoke.

"Have you got a candle?" she asked. "Anything to make a single, open flame?"

"I've got a lamp," he said.

"Would you light it?" she said. "Leave it where it is. Just light it."

He got up and went to the lamp, which was sitting on the table where he had been working, back in a corner—out of line of shot with the window, just in case. He got the incense lighter and sparked the lamp wick aflame. Such was the dullness of the day outside and the shadows of the corner where the table sat, that a visible brightness was added to that part of the room.

"Come back here now," Eileen said. He came back and sat down on the bed with her. "Hold my hand again."

He took it in his own. She lifted her free hand slightly from the blanket and pointed a slim forefinger at the burning lamp, speaking softly:

> "Tiny oil flame, little light,
> "Wax and grow; make pictures bright . . ."

Watching the burning lamp with her, Chaz for a moment saw no difference about it. Then he became aware that its flame was lengthening, stretching up toward the plaster ceiling. It stretched amazingly, broadening and becoming more blue, less yellow, as it did.

It seemed no brighter to look at; but it was doing tricky things to the shadows in that corner of the room. They seemed to shift and mold themselves into forms, even while a sort of general illumination sprang up around them, painting out the familiar dimensions of the corner itself. Unexpectedly—Chaz could not tell when the shift actually occurred—he was no longer looking at the room corner at all, but at some sort of tropical beach where two people were running along side by side on white, hard-packed sand, just beyond the reach of the curling waves. The two people were Eileen and himself.

"Be a monkey's uncle!" muttered Chaz.

"It's true." Eileen sighed with satisfaction beside him. "I've got it all back. That's a scene out of our future, darling; and it's going to be all right."

Chaz reached out mentally for the Mass, suddenly realizing he was no longer blocked off from it, and with its aid opened his mind to the more extended logic-chains that might reach to the future scene Eileen said she was picturing with the candlelight. But he could not find that particular scene himself. Maybe it was somewhere away up there, lost in the unimaginable number of possible futures; but he could not find it. Of course, hadn't she always said her talents were greater than his; and for that matter hadn't she proved it by blocking him off, first from herself and then from the Mass?

On the other hand, wasn't there the possibility that what she was evoking was not a true picture of the future; but a picture of what she hoped the future would be like?

"It's one of the first things little witch girls learn," she was saying now. "To charm a candle flame and make it show pictures."

"Yes," he said.

Finally, just as the day dwindled to its dull close with the pasty face of the clouds glowing bloodshot for a moment on the horizon, a voice called unexpectedly from just below them, in the lower story of the house.

"Red Rover!" it shouted. "It's me, on my way up. Don't shoot."

There were the sounds of boots on the stairs again, ascending this time, and Red Rover walked in, to drop uninvited into the room's single large chair.

"All right," be began. "I—"

He broke off, looking at Eileen sitting up in bed. He bounced to his feet to cross over to her, peered down into her eyes and looked at her neck.

"Well, you were right," he said, glancing at Chaz. He looked back at Eileen. "You're immune."

"I always was," she said.

"Don't act so flip," Rover said, deep in his throat. "There's lots of poor people who prayed to be spared once they were outside here, and weren't."

"Maybe they could have been, though," Chaz said.

"What do you mean?" Rover turned on him.

"I'll show you. Pull your chair up to the table here." Chaz beckoned him into the corner where the table sat. Rover obeyed. "I've fixed you these."

Rover looked at the pieces of paper with the x's, o's, and squares drawn on them. Chaz began to turn them over so that they were blank side up.

"What about them?" Rover asked.

"I want you to try to pick out from the rest all the ones with one kind of symbol," Chaz said.

"Oh, that rhine-stuff," Rover said. "In my neighborhood there were a lot of games like that around. I was never any good at them."

"You hadn't been exposed to the rot, then," said Chaz. "When you were, something like this stopped being a game. Your life was at stake. Since then, things have changed for you. Try it now."

Rover grunted but bent over the slips of paper—now all blank side up. He fingered around among them; and after a minute had twelve slips pulled off to one side.

"By the way," he said, looking up at Chaz. "How many did you say there was of each kind?"

"I didn't say," Chaz answered. "Does it matter?"

Rover shook his head.

"Not if I'm right," he said. "Take a look. I ought to have all the circles. Funny . . ."

Chaz turned over the slips that Rover had pulled aside. They were all marked with the o. He turned up the rest of the slips. There was not an o among the symbols marked on them.

"It's funny, all right," said Rover, frowning at the slips. "I was never any good at those games—never, at all."

"Because you didn't expect to be, then," Chaz said. "Just like the four men who stayed in this house before us. They expected the rot to kill them, and it did; just like you expected to lose, and did."

"Why don't I lose now?"

"Because now your survival instinct has found out you can do something if you want to," Chaz said. "When you were first put out, you must have wanted revenge on whoever or whatever put you out so badly that you didn't spend any time worrying about dying from the rot."

Red Rover nodded slowly. For a moment his face shifted and became faintly savage, then smoothed out again.

"Yes . . ." he said. "That was about it." He looked up at Chaz. "But that still doesn't explain the how of this . . ." He waved at the slips of paper.

"There was a way open your mind could use to keep you alive, if it wanted to," Chaz said. "As I was telling Eileen, earlier, the survival instinct's a pretty primitive mechanism. It doesn't much care about attitudes, or ideas; or really about anything at all, except not dying. When your mind saw a way to keep alive, the survival instinct made it take that way."

"Which was what?"

"You had to believe that you had the paranormal power to defy the rot," said Chaz. "That's what used to puzzle me. The rot's not like a microbe or a virus. It's simply a mechanical thing. The spore finds human lungs a good place to flourish; and it keeps growing until it strangles the person it's inside. Of course, there couldn't be any kind of natural resistance to being choked to death. The rot had to mean one hundred per cent deaths following spore inhalation—there couldn't be any immunes."

"But there are," said Red Rover.

Chaz nodded.

"Myself, the witches—there'd probably be others around in the sterile areas who'd show they were immune if they were ever exposed to the rot—but they take care not to be, just like everyone else, because they don't know yet that they're immune," Chaz said. "The point is, though, both the witches and myself know we've got paranormal powers. The four buried downstairs didn't, or didn't believe they had. But, obviously, you must have, whether you knew it or not. The paranormal powers must have a way of killing or destroying any spores inhaled. As I say, my guess is that you were probably concentrating pretty hard on killing somebody, that first year or so you were outside."

"Yes," said Red Rover. He took a deep breath and sat back in his chair. "But now we know about me and those powers —where do we go from here?"

"We'll get to that," said Chaz. "But first you've got a few things to tell us. To start off with, how did you happen to come here hunting Eileen?"

"I was working for the Citadel," said Rover. "I didn't know she was an immune, of course, or I'd never have taken the job—either that, or I'd have let her know right away what I was doing. But they hired me to tail her until she was dead, then come back and tell them about it."

He looked over at Eileen.

"Sorry . . . Eileen, isn't it?" he said. "But one of the ways I've made a go of it out here has been doing jobs for the Citadel. If you knew—"

"It happens I do know about working for them," said Eileen. "Don't apologize."

"Just how have you been making a go of it?" Chaz asked. "And how much of a go was it?"

Rover told them. He had been a member of a trade rare in present times—a high-rise construction worker. As a result, he had been required to work outside of the sterile areas on those rare occasions when construction or repair was being done in the Chicago area. When he had come back inside from work one day, a routine check had shown his sterile suit to have a leak in it. He had not even been allowed back through the inner airlock to gather his possessions. He had simply been turned loose as he was.

He had been filled with fury at the people who had locked him out. For a year he had lived any way he could outside, with only one thing on his mind—getting back in and getting his hands on the inspector who had ordered him left outside. At the end of that year, he had suddenly realized that he knew nobody else who had survived the rot more than a few months once they had been exiled.

At that time, there were other exiles who had some idea of how long he had been outside; since he had never made any particular secret of it. He got word that some of these were beginning to wonder about him. There were rumors that he was a spy from inside, who had some secret drug to keep him safe from the rot. He learned there was talk of torturing him until he shared the drug and its secret with the rest of them.

He slipped away and holed up; kept out of sight of anyone else for three months to make sure all who knew him were dead. Then he painted himself with imitation neck ulcers

and began to mingle with the new crop of exiles that had
grown up.

There were no further questions about him; until one day
when he ran into a pack of Rovers—as the loose associations
of exiles were called; those who banded together to make
easier the search for food and shelter until the rot got them.
The leader of this particular pack, however, was a man Red
Rover recognized from a year before—and who recognized
him in return. They got together privately and there was a
grim moment in which Red Rover thought it was a case of
kill or be killed. But he learned then that while immunes
were rare, they were not unknown—to other immunes, that
was. Only, it was unwise for them to band together, for fear
of being identified by the other exiles for what they were.
Also, there was an advantage in each leading his own Rover
pack and getting the best of what the pack could provide.

Nonetheless, the immunes kept in touch with each other.
It was through the others that Red Rover had learned that
the Citadel had jobs for exiles willing to work for it; and
would pay for that work in food or comforts impossible to
find outside. Most of the work involved transporting stolen
or illegal goods by outside routes from one sterile area to another. Nearly all the exiles working for the Citadel at any one
time, Red Rover told Chaz and Eileen, were immunes—although the Citadel was never allowed to find this out. The
immune exiles were bitter about all the people still safely in
the sterile areas—but most of all they hated the Citadel repre-
sentatives, who treated them like men and women already
dead.

"All right," said Red Rover, winding up his story. "What
about you two?"

Chaz told him. It took the better part of an hour to cover
the whole story with explanations, from the day of the train
wreck until now. Chaz wound up by showing the other the
diary of the four dead men. When he had skimmed through

it, Red Rover sat for a moment with his legs still outstretched, then gave a long whistle and got to his feet.

"So. Four ordinary dead, instead of one immune here; and I helped keep the place untouched for whoever came next. Well, so long friends," he said. "The best of luck to you both."

"You're leaving?" cried Eileen.

"Right!" said Red Rover. "You people are in too deep with too many large-sized enemies for me. I just want to keep alive —I don't even hate that inspector that put me outside, any more."

"Just walking out isn't going to cut you free of us, now," Chaz said.

"Hmm," said Rover. "Maybe you're right. I'm sorry, friends—" His hand slipped in underneath his sweater at his waist and came out holding a hand laser, pointed at Chaz. "If it's got to be a choice between you or me, maybe I better just turn your bodies in."

Chaz's spine prickled, but he kept his voice steady and did not move from where he sat.

"Don't throw away the best chance you've had in years," he said. "You need us a lot worse than we need you. Don't tell me you like living outside here that much. I'm ready to bet you'd do just about anything for the chance to get back and be part of human society again."

Rover stood holding the gun, but he did not move his finger on the firing button.

"All right," he answered. "Tell me how I can do that. But it's going to have to be something good. As I see it, you're both right up against the Citadel; and the Citadel's the most powerful thing there is, nowadays."

"No, it isn't," Chaz said. "The Pritcher Mass is. Whoever controls that, controls everything."

"Thought you told me the Citadel already had control of the Mass?"

"It does," Chaz said. "That's why the Citadel's got to go."

"Go? There's nothing that can touch the Citadel," said Rover.

"Yes, there is," replied Chaz. "The same thing that can always touch whoever's in power and bring it down."

"Oh?" Red Rover looked at him sardonically.

"People," explained Chaz. "Lots of people. All or most of the people, in fact. Tell me something, Red Rover. Suppose the people in the sterile areas of just the Chicago District were given a choice—face the outside and the rot, or get rid of the Citadel. Which do you think they'd take?"

Red Rover put his handgun away.

"Man," he said to Chaz, "you pushed the right buttons. If you're talking about what I think you're talking about—which is facing all those meditating, prayer-pushing fat hypocrites in the sealed areas with the same sort of thing I've been facing for five years—you've made your point. I want to see that happen no matter what comes, if I have to die for it."

CHAPTER THIRTEEN

RED ROVER came back and sat down.

"All right, then," he said. "Now tell me how you're going to shove a choice like that on the insiders—and that better be good, too. Because if anyone else out here knew how to do it, it'd have been done by now."

"That's one of the things I'm counting on," Chaz said. "Do you think you could round up enough Rover packs to give us a couple of hundred men who feel the same way you do about the people inside?"

"Depends what you want them for," Rover said. "Anyway, they wouldn't all be led by immunes. There aren't that many of us."

"They don't all have to have immune leaders," Chaz said. "Just so they're willing to do some fighting if they have to."

"You aren't going to be able to raid the sterile areas and scare the people there into choosing between the Citadel and the outside with two hundred men," Rover said. "Even if two

hundred men could handle about three thousand police—
which is about what they've got, inside."

"I don't want most of the two hundred inside at all," said
Chaz. "They're just to guard things outside while the action
inside is going on."

"Just guard? What about weapons?"

"We'll get them," said Chaz. "Any kind that is needed."

"You will, will you? You seem pretty sure of yourself," said
Red Rover. "All right, if most of the Rover packs are just going
to guard, what are you going to use to scare insiders into
dumping the Citadel?"

"Explosives," said Chaz. He turned and went over to the
table for a sheet of paper which he brought back and handed
to Rover. "I'm no artist, but that's a rough sketch of the
sealed areas of Chicago as I know them. It looks to me as if
eight large holes blown in the walls and tunnels I've marked
would open up better than half the city to outside and the
rot spores."

"It might," said Rover, studying the sheet. "But you've got
to be talking about *big* holes. Holes you could walk a whole
marching band through. And that's going to take something
like you've never seen in the way of explosives. The few sticks
of overage dynamite or blasting powder we can scrounge up
outside here won't begin to open even one of your holes."

"Don't worry," Chaz said. "We'll get the explosives from
inside. All we need, just like with the weapons."

"From where?"

Chaz nodded at Eileen.

"The covens will help."

"Covens?" Rover echoed, looking at her.

"Witches get together in covens," Eileen said from the
bed. She was beginning to get some normal color back in her
face, after the drawn look that the fever had given her. "Something like Rovers get together in packs. I'm a witch."

"Witch?" said Rover. He blinked at her. "You don't mean
. . . witch?"

"Why not?" said Eileen, smiling a little wickedly at him. "You're a witch, too—or as good as. Remember what you did with those pieces of paper just now? Otherwise you'd never have been immune to the rot. Why, you aren't prejudiced against witches, are you?"

"Well . . . of course not," said Rover. "I was just thinking, that's all. It's the other immunes. What I mean is, maybe we better not rush them. Suppose I just start talking about some people inside who're against putting outside every poor wonker who might have breathed unsterile air for a minute." He became brisk. "Now, how do you plan to do this?"

He turned his attention back to Chaz.

"Eileen knows where the Citadel people are—in a building actually called the Citadel," said Chaz. "Some of us attack that at the same time as one hole is blown in a single sterile area, as a warning. Meanwhile, another bunch—the witches, maybe—have gotten their hands on the city's emergency channel on the viz-phones. They cut in on the general alert following the explosion and broadcast a warning that the rest of Chicago gets opened up unless the Citadel people are handed over to the outsiders. Then they switch to phoning pictures of us taking over the Citadel building and also to film the mobs that form to help us."

"And what," said Red Rover, "are the Chicago city government and police going to be doing while all this is going on?"

"You ought to know better than that," Eileen put in from the bed. "The Citadel owns the Chicago District government. The District Director, the General of Police, and nearly everyone else that counts, are Citadel members—just like with every other large city district in the world. In fact it's not just Chicago. The whole world, more or less, is run from that Citadel building."

Red Rover grunted, as if someone had punched him in the stomach.

"Want to back out?" Chaz asked, watching him closely.

Rover shook his head.

"I guess you want our Rover packs to guard the explosive positions outside the walls and tunnels then," he said.

"That's right," Chaz said. "And set them off only when ordered—if ordered—by you. We can't trust anyone else outside."

"That's true enough." Without actually moving, Rover gave the impression of shaking himself off, like someone coming up into the air after a deep dive underwater. "Now what?"

"Next," Chaz said, "we get together with the covens. Eileen contacted one of the witches in her own coven this afternoon. The whole coven will get us inside and meet with us, as soon as we can come in. What's the closest airlock to the Chicago District?"

"About five miles east," Rover said. "There is a trash disposal lock. We can walk it in a couple of hours. Night's the safe time to move around—if Eileen there's up to it. I've got a portable limpet light."

"I'm up to it," said Eileen.

It was actually closer to four hours before they all sat together in a witches' hole in one of the sterile areas with those members of Eileen's coven who could be gathered together on such short notice. Noticeably among the missing were the Gray Man and one or two others not trusted by the coven.

Chaz introduced Red Rover and once more explained his plan.

"You know," said a white-haired man among the witches, "we're not fighters; and we've got a responsibility to protect the sisterhood and the brotherhood. But we could get your Rovers anything they need—it's our people, not the Citadel's, who control the supply tunnels. And we can probably dig up some of us who know something about the use of explosives for demolition and things like that."

"How about people to man the phones and get what we're doing on the viz-screens?" Chaz asked. The white-haired man hesitated.

"Maybe some of the younger ones might want to take an

active part in that end of it," he said. "We'll know after we check with the other Chicago covens. That'll take several days. Now, about payment for our part in this—"

"Payment!" said Red Rover. The word came out of him with the abrupt, brutal sound of an obscenity.

"I'm sorry," said the witch, looking from Rover to Chaz. "But as I say we've got to protect ourselves and the coming generations of witches. That's been our rule down the centuries."

"Damn you," said Red Rover. "This isn't the Middle Ages any more. You're some sort of psychological types it says in the textbooks, not boogiemen."

"I'm sorry," the white-haired man said again. "But we can't suddenly scrap the rules that we've lived by this long." He kept his gaze on Chaz. "When the Citadel's influence is cleaned out of the Pritcher Mass, we want the witches to take over control of it. I don't mean control out on the Mass itself; I mean the Earth end of it, the policy and decision-making authority back here. We can't risk having the Mass used against us."

"You sure you can speak for all your friends?" demanded Rover, before Chaz could answer.

"Sure enough so that I know there's no use going to them for help unless you can promise what I'm asking." The witch answered without taking his eyes off Chaz. "Well?"

"Well . . ." said Chaz, slowly. "I'll agree—provided one thing. No one with paranormal talents is to be excluded from the witch group that gets control of the Earth end of the Mass."

"That's reasonable enough," said the witch. "All right. We'll get busy."

Arrangements were made for delivery of explosives and other supplies to the Rovers by the witches, and the meeting broke up. Chaz, Eileen, and Red Rover were conducted back outside by the same route they had been let in, through the service airlock of a waste-disposal outlet. With dawn only a few hours away, they headed back to the house.

"What makes you think you can deliver control of the Mass to anyone, once this is over?" Red Rover asked Chaz bluntly. Chaz looked at him in the illumination from the limpet light the other man was carrying.

"Do you trust me?" Chaz asked. "Or don't you?"

"Oh, I trust you," Rover said. "I'll also look you up afterward and kill you, if it turns out trusting you was the wrong thing to do."

It took better than a week—both inside and outside the sterile areas of Chicago—to set things up. In the meantime, Red Rover left a note just outside the airlock that was his contact point with the Citadel, saying that Eileen had died of the rot. Two days later, checking the point from under cover, he saw the red piece of cloth lying on the ground that was the signal that he was wanted. He waited until after dark, went in without a light and found an answering note. He took it a safe distance away over a hill to use a light on it, and read that he was to produce Eileen's body and bring word of the location of a man answering Chaz's description. Dousing his light, he carefully took the note back and left it where he had found it, by the red cloth. From then on he stayed clear of the contact point.

Meanwhile, however, the covens had picked up word that the top people in the Citadel organization were returning from around the world, and even from the Mass, to meet at the Citadel building in Chicago. An unhappy and fearful male witch slipped outside the sterile areas to bring the news to Chaz personally.

"I expected it," Chaz told the man. "They've got the Mass and, as Eileen herself reminded me once, people with paranormal talents and computers. They can follow logic-chains well enough to see that I'm going to try something against them. Naturally they're getting together to plan strategy."

"If they know that much," said the witch, "they may know

just what we're planning to do. They can be waiting for us."

"They don't know," Chaz said. "They can't predict correctly without having all relevant facts. And they don't."

"What don't they know?"

"Certain things," said Chaz. "For one, that there are immunes among the exiles; and that these immunes owe their lives to paranormal powers they didn't even suspect they had."

The witch man stared at him.

"What else don't they know?" he asked at last.

"Some things," Chaz said. "I'll tell you what your people can do, though. You can pull out of this if you want to. Only, if we lose, the Citadel is going to trace those supplies back to help from your covens; and if we win, you won't get the authority over the Pritcher Mass you wanted."

The witch left. But there was no talk from the covens of withdrawing their assistance in the few days that remained.

The attack on the Citadel had been planned for a Sunday afternoon. At three that afternoon, Chaz, Eileen, Red Rover, and a dozen of the Rovers, about half of them immunes, were waiting in the supply tunnel that connected with the Citadel building. Chaz was carrying a portable phone to the cable in the tunnel wall; and he had it keyed to show the southern face of the building and the sky over the western section of the Lower Loop sterile area of Chicago. The view was from the pickup of a public phone booth in the square before the south side of the building, which was listed in the District Directory simply as the "Embry Tower." It was one of the eighty-story towers raised in that part of Chicago in the 1990s, shortly before the rot had appeared. It poked its top thirty stories through the upper protective dome over the sterile area like a weed stem through a gas bubble in swamp water; and its outer glass facing reflected the gray clouds overhead with a matching grayness of its own. There were only a few casual pedestrians crossing through the square at the moment. Half a dozen non-uniformed guards could also be seen playing the part of casual idlers, within the transparent walls of the street-level lobby of the tower.

"There!" said Chaz; and the rest of those with him crowded closer to the small phone screen for a look. A black plume of smoke was rising toward the clouds off to the west beyond the tops of the area's buildings. A second later, the tunnel about them shuddered slightly with a shock wave.

The scene on the phone screen was suddenly replaced by the picture of a middle-aged, heavy-featured woman wearing a green police uniform. The sharp warning whistle of the emergency signal sounded. If Chaz's phone had not already been in use, that signal would have activated it.

"Citizens of the Lower Loop Area," said the woman on the screen. "Emergency. I repeat, this is an emergency broadcast under the pollution warning system. All citizens of the Lower Loop area, please pay special attention. All citizens of the nineteen sterile areas of the main Chicago District, pay close attention. An as-yet-unexplained explosion has breached the seal in the western extremity of the Lower Loop area. All available pollution-fighting equipment has been called in from all nineteen areas; and a chemical barrier is being thrown up while a temporary seal is under construction behind the exposed area.

"All citizens are warned to stay where they are, if possible, and preserve local sterile conditions. Please, those of you who may have relatives or friends in the area of the explosion, stay away. Repeat, *stay away!* Crowding the access routes to the area will only increase the danger of polluting the whole Lower Loop. All care will be taken to ensure that those not exposed will not be left beyond the temporary seal when it is locked in place. I repeat, do not crowd the area. All care will be taken—"

The image of the woman in the uniform coat was suddenly wiped off the screen, to be replaced by a figure in an ordinary gray jumpsuit wearing a flexmask—and it was impossible to tell from the screen whether it was a man or woman. The

accompanying voice was similarly disguised by a filter, so that
the anonymity of its sex was complete. It was one of the
witches, Chaz guessed; but which one probably even Eileen
would never know.

"Attention, citizens of all Chicago sterile areas," said the
figure. "Attention, all Chicago citizens. The explosion just
announced by pollution-control authorities was not an accident. I repeat, not an accident. The security of the Lower
Loop areas has been deliberately breached as a warning to
Chicago citizens. All other areas in the main Chicago District will be similarly breached, and the citizens now in them
exposed to the rot spores, if the members of the criminal
organization known as the Citadel, who are now occupying
the Embry Tower in the Lower Loop, are not immediately
removed from that building and put outside the sterile areas.

"I repeat. The members of the Citadel now in the Embry
Tower must be removed and placed outside the sterile areas.
They must be put out at the spot where the Lower Loop
was just breached, before sunset, or the other areas of the
main Chicago District will be breached in similar manner.
We, the Committee for the Purification of Chicago, call on
all citizens to assist in securing these criminals and seeing
that they are put outside.

"I will repeat again what I have said. The breach of the
Lower Loop area was not an accident. Other areas will be
breached unless the criminals of the Citadel are removed
from Embry Tower and placed outside by sunset. We, the
Committee for the Purification of Chicago, call on all citizens
to assist in securing these criminals—"

"Let's go," said Chaz, turning from the phone to the door
near by, leading into the basement of the Embry Tower. He
fitted a vibration key to the lock plate and the heavy door
swung open. Inside, in a small room at the foot of the concrete staircase, were three uniformed guards—all sound asleep
in chairs.

Chaz grinned at Eileen. The tension of the moment already had the body adrenalin singing in his blood.

"Beautiful, honey," he said. "I had to see it to believe it—a spell cast through a cased-steel door."

"Physical barriers don't matter. But it's odd these two weren't warded like the outer lobby guards. The Citadel's got enough witch renegades like the Gray Man—" Eileen broke off, glancing up the empty stairs. "Chaz!"

"What's wrong?" He swung about to stare at the harmless-looking stairs.

"Power," Eileen said, unhappily. "Someone with a terrible lot of power, up there somewhere. Can't you feel it?"

Chaz tried, felt nothing, reached for help from the Mass, tried again and still felt nothing. He shook his head.

"You mean somebody knows we're coming?"

"I . . . don't think so," said Eileen. "But whoever it is, he's the most powerful person I've ever felt."

"He?"

"I don't know. It just feels male, somehow . . ."

Chaz shook his head.

"Forget it. We can't fiddle around now." He spoke over his shoulder to the rest of them. "Come on."

He led the way up the staircase. At the fire door of the street-level landing, Red Rover snapped to the men just behind him.

"Seal that!"

Several Rovers stopped and began to melt the edges of the door into its heavy metal frame with their hand lasers. Chaz continued up the stairs.

At each landing, Red Rover left men at work sealing the fire doors. But four landings up the staircase itself ended, abruptly and in violation of all fire ordinances. A solid concrete wall barred their way.

"The elevators," Chaz said.

He went through the nearby fire door into what seemed to be a fourth-floor landing. There were some doors opening on

the landing, all ajar, all showing small, empty offices. The
elevator tubes were there also, but they were halted, their
floating discs hanging frozen in the transparent tubes.

"Think they expected us, after all?" Red Rover asked.

"Maybe," said Chaz. "Maybe just an automatic protective
reaction switched them off when the emergency phone
broadcast came on, or the guards down in the lobby found
out we were here."

Below them, up the stairwell, they could hear a crackling
noise as the lobby guards, alerted by the heat radiating from
the half-melted edges of the sealed fire door at that level,
were now trying to cut through the door from their own side.
Luckily it was easier to seal a door with a laser than open it
with such a weapon, after it was sealed.

"What now?" Rover said.

"I thought of something like this," Chaz said. "Eileen's
been held in this building before. She's got a memory of the
room she was kept in. If she and I can transfer to that room,
maybe we can get the elevators going for the rest of you.
Give me the recorder and the suit bag."

He reached out, and the Rover with the portable phone
recorder, slung like a satchel from one shoulder, lifted it off
and passed it to him. Chaz slung the strap over his own
right shoulder and turned to Eileen. He took the suit bag
another Rover passed him and produced a pair of airsuits,
handing one to Eileen.

"What's that for?" Red Rover asked. Chaz did not take
time to answer until he and Eileen were both suited up. He
watched Eileen close her faceplate, then turned to Rover
before sealing his own.

"I'll try taking her out to the Mass and back in again," he
said. "It worked in rehearsal, but then we both knew where
we wanted to come back to. If it doesn't work this time,
take your Rovers back out and mingle with whatever crowd
shows up in the square. Give us five minutes, then leave.
But keep your portable phone open for any word from me.

These suits don't have any phones of their own. All right?"

"Right enough," said Red Rover.

Chaz reached with his gloved hand for Eileen's. He winked at her through his faceplate, in silent signal.

The landing around them blinked out. There was a glimpse of starlight and the Mass platform apparently standing up vertically alongside them to their right, then they were in what looked like an ordinary, condominium one-room apartment.

Chaz looked at Eileen. She was nodding and smiling through her faceplate as she unsealed it so that he could hear her speak. He reached up and unsealed his own.

As he pulled it open to the room air, a sudden dizziness took him. He opened his mouth to shout a warning at Eileen; but saw her with her own suit unsealed and already falling. A moment of disorientation took him. . . .

He opened his eyes to find himself out of the airsuit entirely and seated in a chair.

Eileen was seated in a chair alongside him. They were under the dome of a roof garden—almost certainly on the top floor of the Embry Tower. Facing them were several tables pushed together to make one long surface; and behind this sat a handful of people, among whom Chaz recognized Waka, Ethrya, and Jai.

Beside Chaz, Eileen made a small, choking noise. He looked quickly at her, and saw her staring at Jai in either fascination or terror.

"You?" she said, in a strangled voice. "You're the one I felt downstairs?"

"Yes," said Jai. "And thank you, sister. I take the recognition as a compliment. You seem to have more than an ordinary share of the talent yourself."

CHAPTER FOURTEEN

CHAZ THROTTLED back the dismay and fury that rose inside him. It was strangely easy to do. Suddenly he felt almost indifferent to the situation.

"You're one of the Citadel crew, too, then," he said calmly to Jai. "Or maybe you're their head man?"

"No one in the Citadel is head man," answered Jai. "We're like any business, in our organization. You might compare me to a Chairman of the Board, if you want to make a comparison. Ethrya, here, would be President of the company, perhaps."

The tall man's voice was as gentle as ever. Chaz shook his head a little.

"What could an outfit like this offer someone like you?" he said. "Particularly if you've got the paranormal abilities Eileen says you have."

"Freedom," said Jai, gently. "Some people find freedom by getting well away from others. I find it by being well in con-

trol of others." He looked at Chaz almost sadly. "That's always been your own one flaw, Chaz. You don't have the drive
to control others yourself; but at the same time you refuse
to let others have any control over you. That's why I've voted
against you finally; even if I was for your coming out to the
Mass, originally."

He glanced to his right at Waka.

"Not everybody agreed with me about that," he said.
"Poor old Alex here was caught in the middle."

"Why take chances?" Ethrya said. "It was a real chance
you took when you had Waka qualify him for the Mass. If
we'd killed him in the first place the way *I* said, he wouldn't
have been around to cause us even the trouble he's causing
us now."

"Investment theory," said Jai. "The whole theory of investment assumes some risk-taking in order to get the chance of
making a greater profit. Chaz might have paid off for us very
well. Besides, the present situation is under control."

He looked away from Ethrya over to one side where a
couple of men were setting up two antennae, each about
three meters tall, and two meters apart. For a moment they
stood there unenergized, like silvery wands; and then a two-
dimensional image sprang into being between them. It was
a view of the square before the south side of the Tower,
picked up apparently by a camera high on the building's
side, but telescopically enlarged to give close-ups from what
seemed to be a few feet above the heads of those in the
square.

Meanwhile, people behind the long table section were
changing seats. Ethrya was giving up her chair beside Jai
to a heavy-set man in his fifties with a bulldog face; a man
who looked vaguely familiar. Chaz stared at him for a moment before it registered on him that he was looking at the
Director for the Chicago District. Eileen had been right
about the Citadel's involvement with government officials.

Chaz looked back at the scene in the square below. *Think,*

he commanded himself. The square was beginning to fill up with a crowd that was clearly disturbed and unfriendly in its attitude toward the Embry Tower building. Chaz glimpsed several of the Rovers he recognized, wearing ordinary jumpsuits, circulating among the crowd and clearly talking its emotions up. He did not, however, recognize Red Rover anywhere. Strangely the absence of the immune leader raised only a small, unimportant feeling of curiosity in him. . . . He remembered Eileen and looked over at her.

She was sitting in a chair just like his, not more than three meters from him. She smiled a little palely, as their eyes met. Like him, she was not tied in the chair or restrained in any way; although, looking beyond her, out by the far end of the long table surface, he saw a thin young man covering them both with a hand laser.

Chaz turned his head back to the table.

"Jai?" he said.

The tall man broke off a low-voiced conversation with the Chicago District Director and a short, white-haired man standing behind them. The white-haired man turned and went off to take a chair several seats down the table to Jai's right. Jai looked at Chaz. Chaz had to think for a second. Then he remembered why he had called the tall man.

"Eileen," said Chaz. "You don't need her here."

Jai shook his head.

"To tell the truth, I'd like to do without her myself," he said. "After all, I'm a witch, too—or was. And hurting people except in self-defense is bad for the talent. It builds up callouses on the sensitivity areas. But in this case we have to make a case against you, Chaz; and we need her for that. A shame—" He glanced at Eileen for a moment. "You really do have an unusual talent, sister."

"Don't call me sister," said Eileen emotionlessly. "You don't deserve the name of witch, if you ever did. . . . *Dark see you, dark blind you/ grave take you, curse bind you.*"

"I'm sorry," said Jai, very gently indeed. "I understand how you feel. But you ought to know better than to think you can hurt me in any way with the Craft. In all my life I never found anyone who could approach me at its use; much less one able to attack me with it."

He turned back to talking with the District Director. In the screen, the square was now packed with people; and to the west the dark stain of smoke from fires following the explosion still hung like a dirty finger smudge on the sky above the city's buildings and transparent domes. It was getting on now toward four o'clock, Chaz guessed; and the gray-clouded early winter day, as it always did at this hour, had become dull-lighted and heavy with a chilling dreariness. Something inside him was telling him that the battle was already lost. Lost and forgotten . . .

A bit from a memory floated out of the back of Chaz's mental attic into the front of his mind. A query in a poem. What was it from? Oh, yes . . . *"La Belle Dame sans Merci,"* by John Keats. . . .

> *"O, what can ail thee, knight-at-arms,*
> *"Alone and palely loitering?*
> *"The sedge is wither'd from the lake,*
> *"And no birds sing. . . ."*

And then, in the third from the last stanza, the answer.

> *". . . la belle Dame sans Merci hath thee in thrall!"*

—Only it was not La Belle Dame, in this instance but Le Beau Jai, who had Eileen and himself in thrall. . . .

Faintly, from a sound receiver somewhere, he heard a chanting. He looked at the image of the square below, and saw the crowd swaying back and forth like one person. Obviously, it was the source of the chanting, which was directed against the Embry Tower; but the receiver was set at such low volume he could not make out what words were being chanted. The sound and swaying stopped then, almost abruptly; and the camera view swung around to look awkwardly down at a narrow angle on the lower front of the building itself. On the lower building side there was now an image of the long table and those seated behind it; with the central focus on the face of the Chicago District Director. He began to speak. Someone turned the volume up on the receiver and it echoed his words as they also reached Chaz's ears from directly across the little distance between him and the long table.

". . . realize that it is unusual for myself, as District Director, to address you all over an emergency phone broadcast this way. However, we are presently faced with a situation in which the utmost in self-restraint and control will be needed from all our citizens. As most of you already know, saboteurs from outside the sterile areas have succeeded in blowing a hole in the protection of the Lower Loop. As anyone might expect, we neither judge nor condemn these sick-minded who have had to be removed from the sterile community for the greater good of all. But for that same greater good, we must now take defensive measures to protect our healthy populace. In order that all our Chicago District citizens should understand the need for such defensive measures, I have felt it needful to acquaint you not only with a plot that has already resulted in one explosion, plus the threat of others that would indeed pose a danger to us all, but also to acquaint you with the chief saboteurs and events leading up to this criminal act."

He paused, glancing at the image of the square below. Chaz also looked. Judging from the reaction of the crowd, most of them were paying attention. It was a good bet, thought Chaz absently, that all through the Chicago areas, most of the others there were listening as well.

"These saboteurs," the Director went on, "have attempted to blackmail you all into exiling some perfectly innocent and valuable members of the sterile community. Their aim in

this was to cripple a scientific project which is dear to the
spiritual and ethical hopes of all our people, in that it offers
hope—not to us, but to some chosen few of our children—
who with its help may one day find a new Earth on a clean,
untouched world; and by avoiding the mistakes of our prof-
ligate ancestors, set the human race once more on its upward
road.

"But before I say any more, let me take a moment to reassure everyone that our police, acting on information supplied by citizens who were approached by the saboteurs but
who took their information immediately to the authorities,
have located all four of the other explosion sites prepared by
the saboteurs—"

"That can't be right," said Chaz out loud, without thinking. "No one inside the sterile areas knew the number or location of the other sites; and only one man outside, besides
myself, knew until three hours ago."

"—I will now turn you over to Police Central on remote
for a report by the General of Police himself," said the Director hastily, and sat back in his chair, turning to Jai. "Did they
hear him?"

Jai looked past Chaz. Chaz, turning, saw a red-haired,
bulky man at a small table bearing commercial-sized broadcast recorders. The bulky man shook his head and walked
up, past Chaz, to the table.

"No chance," he told Jai and the Director. "I've got his
chair in a dead zone. I can feed him into the screen with a
directional pickup at any time you want. When I do that,
he'll be seen and heard until I feed him out, again. Outside
of that, he's simply not here to the equipment."

"How long are you giving the General of Police?" asked
the Director, looking at his watch.

"Four minutes," said the bulky man. "Then we return to
you and you do the introduction to the Assistant Director
from the Mass here." He nodded at Jai. "While we've got a
moment, though, Mr. Director, if you'd move your chair a

little closer to the Assistant Director's, it'd help in the reaction shots. We want to close in on your face, looking concerned, when he makes his more important points. He'll hold
up one forefinger a bit to signal us; then I'll signal you, Mr.
Director, and you listen for the line you want to react to . . ."

Chaz let his attention drift from the conversation at the
table. He looked at Eileen and smiled; and once more she
managed a smile in return. The thin young man covering
them with the laser continued alert.

Chaz's mind had been working slowly with the situation,
trying to lay out logic-chains on the possibilities. But he
found himself unable to hold the chains in his mind. It was
hard to concentrate in the face of the realization that everything was all over. For himself, he thought, it hardly mattered. Nobody would mourn him after he was dead; and as
for the dying itself, that hardly mattered more to him than
his death would to anyone else. He had been something like
a cornered rat in his reactions all his life; and in a way he had
always been prepared for the time when the rest of the
world would turn on him and destroy him. He knew that
whenever his own time came he would go out in a red rage;
which was not the worst way to die, no matter what was
being done to you at the time. But, of course, there was
Eileen. Jai was clearly planning that she should share whatever conclusion was in store for Chaz; and she would not find
dying such an indifferent matter as he did—especially if it
was some kind of prolonged death.

He looked at the man with the laser and put his hand on
the edge of the chair seat, under him. Maybe by throwing
the chair at the thin young man he could distract the gunman long enough to reach him and get the weapon away.
Then he might be able to live long enough to shoot Eileen.
She would not be expecting it and from him; it would be
mercifully swift. She would never know what hit her.

". . . Now that you have all heard what the General of
Police has had to say . . ." The City Director was talking

again. "I want to introduce you to a man some of you may already have recognized in the group shots of this table—Jai Losser, Assistant Director on the Pritcher Mass. To those of you who are surprised to find the Assistant Director of the Mass back here on Earth, I should explain something that has been a closely guarded official secret, and which is revealed now only because of the seriousness of the situation. This building, the Embry Tower, which the saboteurs would have had you believe contained the chief members of the reputed criminal organization popularly named the Citadel, is actually the confidential headquarters on Earth for work with the Pritcher Mass. Assistant Director Losser is now going to speak to you because the chief saboteur, whom we have under arrest here, together with the woman who was his first assistant, was himself a worker on the Mass. . . . Mr. Losser."

Jai leaned forward, smiling softly, as the City Director sat back in his chair.

"I'm honored to speak to the citizens of Chicago District," he said pleasantly, "although I wish the occasion was a happier one. The chief saboteur the City Director mentioned is a man named Charles Roumi Sant, formerly employed in this District, and a man whom I regret to say I once liked; and of whom I had a very high opinion."

He gestured with one hand toward Chaz. Chaz, watching the image between the two upright antennae, saw his own face appear many times lifesize on the south face of the Embry Tower. It showed there only a minute, then was replaced by a brief close-up of the District Director, showing concern on his features, followed by a return to a head-and-shoulder shot of Jai.

"Even now," Jai said, "I hate to condemn this man; although tests show him to be completely sane and responsible —and it is hard to believe that any sane man could plan on exposing hundreds of thousands of Chicago residents to the rot, simply to gain a position on the Pritcher Mass that would ensure his being one of those that would emigrate to a new world; once such a world had been found."

He waved again at Chaz. Once more, Chaz saw his own face flashed on the building. The sound of the crowd voices mounted. Jai's features replaced those of Chaz.

"The details are somewhat technical," Jai said. "Briefly, however, Sant tried to gain a position of authority on the Mass by creating an illusion that he had contacted not only a habitable world, but the intelligent aliens on it. This hoax was exposed when I went out with him during a shift of work on the Mass; and made mental contact with the illusion myself. While it first seemed to have some validity, a closer examination showed nothing really new or alien about the world or its so-called alien inhabitants. Working with an artist, I have managed to produce actual-size representations of those aliens as Sant imagined them. I have those representations here; and you will be shown them. Notice how they are nothing but a common Earth insect, and an equally common Earth mollusk, enlarged."

He waved his hand to the left side of the table; and Chaz, looking, saw two large two-dimensional cut-out sort of figures. One was very much like the Mantis and one very much like a large Snail, from the cartoon world. He looked back at Jai.

"I didn't know you were with me," he said to Jai. "You actually are good, aren't you? But why drag that part in— Wait, I understand. You've got to find some way of justifying what happens to me to the non-Citadel people back on the Mass. You've got to have some reason for shutting off the contact with the cartoon world I added to the Mass."

Jai did not answer. He had paused to let his viewers look at the representations. Now, he went on.

"When I told Sant I knew this was a hoax," Jai said, "he admitted it, but begged to be kept on at the Mass. I was forced to refuse. He came back to Earth. Back here, he went outside the Chicago District and gathered a crew of saboteurs with the idea of blackmailing the citizens of Chicago into creating a threat to this building and its workers. It was his hope that he could use that threat in turn to blackmail us here into putting him back on the Mass in a position of authority."

Jai paused and smiled across the table at Chaz. For a second Chaz saw his own face, looking oddly unconcerned, imaged on the building in the screen between the antennae. Then Jai was back on the screen.

"But we," said Jai, "trusting in the good common sense of our Chicago citizens, decided to call his bluff; with the result that, as the General of Police has explained, we have now nullified all his attempts at sabotage; and he, with the woman who abetted him, is now in custody."

Another flash of Chaz's face on the building below. The volume of sound from outside was turned up; and the voice of the crowd was an ugly voice, becoming uglier at the sight of Chaz's image.

"Sant and the woman will now be sent under police escort from this building through the streets to Police Central," Jai said. "You may all return to your homes, satisfied that everything is secure and justice will be done. Please, I beg you, any of you who have strong feelings about what Sant might have succeeded in doing, take my word for it that in our courts justice will indeed be done. Do not be tempted to take it into your own hands. . . ."

The crowd roared like a senseless beast.

"I trust you," said Jai, with a sad smile, "your General of Police and your District Director trust you, to allow these criminals and the two police officers who will be escorting them, to proceed in an orderly manner from here to Police Central—"

Chaz rose with a great effort and threw his chair at the young man with the laser, knocking him down. Following the chair as fast as he could—but it was almost as if he moved in slow motion—Chaz was on top of the gunman before the man could recover, and had his hands on the weapon. But before he could get to his feet a number of people were holding him. He was pushed to his knees and the laser wrested easily out of his grasp. He was hauled to his feet again by two men in police uniforms. They marched him back to his chair, shoved him down into it, and let him go. He sagged there, feeling too heavy to move.

"Not Eileen . . ." he said to Jai, in dull protest. The sound of his voice roared back at him from the screen; and he realized that he had probably been imaged there ever since he had picked up his chair to throw it at the man with the laser.

Jai came around the table. The handsome face bent down to him; and Jai's voice also echoed from the screen, speaking not merely to Chaz, but to the crowd below as well.

"I'm afraid so, Sant," said Jai, sadly. "Your accomplice, like you, is going to have to face justice for the way both of you have threatened innocent lives."

Jai smiled gently, regretfully. One of the lines from Keats' poem came floating back into Chaz's mind, with changes.

". . . Le beau Jai sans Merci, hath thee in . . ."

With that, at last, understanding broke through the thick pressure clouding Chaz's mind. Abruptly he realized what was happening; and on the heels of that realization came immediate reaction.

—So it was that the red fury he had expected at the end finally exploded within Chaz. It was then, in the ultimate moment, that he went berserk.

CHAPTER FIFTEEN

—But not by the simple, physical route alone. His causes had been larger than that.

They were all he had suffered under, erupting within him at once. The sad hypocrisy of his aunt and cousins, the stifling closeness of domed streets and sealed buildings, the oppression of a race that seemed to sit with folded hands, waiting for its end. All this, plus his own loneliness, his own rebellion, his one gain of someone who actually loved him, in Eileen—whom Jai had been planning to include in Chaz's destruction at the hands of a deluded mob, while Chaz sat by, bewitched out of courage and sense.

Chaz reached for the Mass on Earth, as he had found it when he had hung above the platform beyond Pluto, wanting to return to Eileen on Earth. Once more he touched it and drew strength from it. With that strength, he threw off the dead weight of hopelessness that Jai's Craft had laid on him; as easily as throwing off a passing touch of drowsiness when there was work needing to be done. . . . Almost, he had been ready to go to the mob like a lamb to the butchers.

His head woke. It went light and clear; and suddenly things seemed very obvious and very easy to do. Ignoring the thin individual who was again holding the laser on him, he got up once more from his chair—but this time it was everybody else who seemed to be in slow motion as they reacted to his moving—turned, and went back to the table with the camera and recording equipment. He brushed the bulky man there easily aside and spoke directly into the equipment.

"Red Rover!" he said. "Blow the other explosive charges. Blow them all, now. Every one."

He heard his voice thunder from the image between the antennae, and caught sight of the man with the laser coming at him, shoving the weapon almost in his face.

"Don't be a damn fool!" he said. "I know you've got orders not to shoot. They want the crowd to get me."

He shoved the thin man away and turned back to the equipment.

"Sorry, People," he said to the people of Chicago District. "But you'd have to face up to the rot, sooner or later. There are more exiles outside all the time. How long do you think it would have been before they began sabotaging the sterile areas on their own?"

He turned away from the equipment and went back to the long table. It was full of people ignoring him; all talking on the phone, ordering buildings to be sealed, rooms to be sealed, hovercraft to pick them up and carry them away from Chicago. Only Jai was not talking. He was watching the others instead, with a sad, dry smile. But he dropped the smile and turned to face Chaz as Chaz came up to him.

"Why?" he said to Chaz. "What good did it do you? Once those other holes are blown in Chicago's sterile defenses nobody will be able to save you from the people, even if anyone wants to."

"Never mind me," said Chaz. "Don't you understand it's

all over? It'll never be business as usual for your group again. Didn't you realize how it was? That I could lose; but there was no way your Citadel could win?"

"I don't know what you're talking about," said Jai.

"The Pritcher Mass," Chaz answered. "It can't do you any good, no matter what happens to me. If you were there with me mentally when I went from the platform Mass to the cartoon world, you have to remember they told us that."

"They?"

Chaz threw his arm out to point at the cut-out figures of the Snail and the Mantis.

"Those?" Jai said, and made a dismissing gesture. "We'll find some other world."

"You'll find—" Chaz stared at him and understanding, even of Jai, woke suddenly in him. "I'll be damned! You're self-brainwashed, too. In spite of all that paranormal talent and intelligence, you've been burying your head in the sand like the rest!"

Jai looked back down at him with a closed face.

"Let me show you something," said Chaz. He reached for the Mass beyond Pluto—and found the way blocked by Jai's mind and paranormal strength. "All right. We can do it right from here."

Chaz turned his mind once more to the Mass on Earth, found it, and reached out through it to the cartoon world, to the Mantis itself and the Snail. He found them, feeling Jai's mind with him, watching.

"They don't want to believe it," Chaz said, at once out loud to Jai and through his mind to the Mantis on the cartoon world. "Can I call on you once more to tell them yourselves that the road to any other world is closed? That there's no place we can escape to?"

"This once more," said the Mantis.

The Mass on Earth stirred and shifted under the transparent bubble roofing the top floor of the Embry Tower; and all over Chicago, reality changed. Not for Chaz and Jai alone, but for everyone there. It was a little change, and at the same time, a big change—as if an extra physical dimension had been added, so that there was no longer merely length, width, and height and duration; but also *away*, binding Earth and the cartoon world together.

The Mantis and a Snail appeared over the city along the *away* dimension. In one sense they were the cardboard cutout figures of themselves, now become solid and alive. In another sense they were enormous, standing in mid-air between building tops and heavy cloud layer, visible to all of Chicago's sterile areas. But in a final sense they were even more than this, because they also stretched from Earth clear back across the unbelievable distance of light years to their own world, where in actuality they still were. And yet, these three things they seemed to be were really only one. Topologically, in the *away* dimension, all three manifestations were only aspects of a single unity—like three views of a torus, the angle of viewing made them look to be one thing, rather than another.

"It's quite true," said the Mantis to everyone in the Chicago District, while the Snail beside him, without moving, slid endlessly over a thin surface of eternally flowing liquid. "There are other worlds; but not for your race, until you can show your right to them."

"You can't stop us," said Jai—and it was a brave statement. With the *away* dimension now visible around them, Jai's talent glowed visibly, like a small sun among the feeble lamps of the other human beings around him. But that glowing was a tiny thing compared to the burning greatness of the Mantis and the Snail.

"We do not stop you," said the Mantis. "We neither aid you nor hinder you. You do it all to yourselves. Think of yourselves for a moment, not as individuals, but as one creature called Human made up of billions of little individual parts. This creature told itself it would build a bridge to the stars; but it lied to itself. What its hands were building, all the time it talked of a new world, was something else it wanted much more."

"What's that?" demanded Jai.

"How do we know?" answered the Mantis. "We are not Human; you are. But we can tell you what you have built is not a way to another world. When the time comes that another planet is what you really want—what you want more than anything else—you will undoubtedly find it. And as we neither helped nor hindered now, we will not help nor hinder then. We would not even be talking to you now, if one of those tiny parts who knows what Human wants had not reached us through what you all built, and put upon us the ethical duty to answer him."

The Mantis looked at Chaz and disappeared. It and the Snail were gone. *Away* was no longer perceptible; and the cut-out figures were only cut-out figures again.

Jai looked at Chaz. In that moment, a dull sound was heard, far off across the city, and a faint shock jarred the floor under their feet.

"There goes one of the explosion points," Chaz said. "Tell me, how many did you really find?"

"Four," said Jai. "But you've just killed several million people in this District. I won't die; and the other witches won't —and at a guess there'll be some others who'll live. We've suspected there were some exiles that had turned out to be immune. But what about the four million in Chicago District who aren't? At least the Citadel would have gone on keeping them alive."

"You call this living?" Chaz said. "Anyway, you're wrong. No one ought to die unless almost everybody goes on refusing to face up to what's happened. The Mantis was right— the Pritcher Mass never was something to take us to a new world."

"Then what was it?" Jai said.

Chaz shook his head, slowly.

"You're blind, Jai," he said, softly. "Self-blinded. How could you live completely inside glass, plastic, and concrete, and never know at all what was outside those things? *'The Earth is the Lord's . . .'* Paul the Apostle wrote to the Corinthians. *'Late on the third day,'* Albert Schweitzer wrote in 1949, *'at the very moment when at sunset we were making our way through a herd of hippopotamuses, there flashed upon my mind, unforseen and unsought, the phrase, "Reverence for Life."* . . . *Now I had found my way to the idea in which affirmation of the world and ethics are contained side by side; now I knew that the ethical acceptance of the world and of life, together with the ideals of civilization contained in this concept, has a foundation in thought . . .'* "

Another faint thud reached their ears and they felt another shudder of the building to a shock wave through the earth below. Jai frowned at him.

"I don't follow you," Jai said. "Are you preaching a set of universal ethics? Because if you are, you really are insane. There's no such thing."

"Yes, there is; and there always has been," answered Chaz. "A set of universal ethics has been with us from the beginning, whether we believed in them or not. Certain responses in living creatures, and particularly in intelligent ones, are hard and firm as physical laws. Why do you think the Mantis and the Snail answered me when I called? They see more laws than we see; and obey more. But we have to obey the ones we can see if we want to survive. If we try to ignore them, we'll become extinct. The responsibility not to foul your own nest is a primitive law. We ignored it; and the rot came."

There was a third sound of explosion.

"We could have beaten the rot by getting away from Earth," said Jai.

"No. If we'd managed to do that, we'd only have blundered again and created another way to destroy ourselves," Chaz said. "Earth's more than just a place to walk on. Back before houses and fire, and even speech, we found food and

shelter and survival in the Earth; and the older part of us re-
members it. That part has been fighting all this time for just
one thing; to get outside, again. Because that—nothing else
—is the road to survival."

"I can't believe it," Jai muttered, almost to himself. "We
built the Pritcher Mass. We aimed it for new worlds."

"*You* built it?" said Chaz. "You and people like you only
oversaw its building. Everyone on Earth built the Mass—
creating it out of the basic, instinctive urge to make something that would destroy the rot, and save Earth, and themselves. You were with me when we met the Mantis and the
Snail before, and you heard what the Mantis said. Also you
saw how I reached them just now. The Pritcher Mass isn't
out on the platform, beyond Pluto. It's here, on Earth."

Jai stared at him.

"It can't be," the tall man said.

"Why not? You ought to remember the Mantis telling me it
was here. What's distance and position to the Mass?" said
Chaz. "It's here on Earth, where it always belonged, with the
people who made it."

"What sort of nonsense is this about the people back here
building the Mass? Not one in three hundred thousand has
talent."

"Of course they have," said Chaz. "Every human being's
got it. Every animal and plant. Fifty years ago they were prov-
ing that plants reacted *before* they were burned or cut. Why
do you think the plants and animals aren't touched by the
rot?"

"Next," said Jai, contemptuously, "you'll be telling me the
rot was created by the mass unconscious of the plants and
animals striking back at the one species that was threatening
their common world."

"Perhaps," said Chaz. "But that part doesn't matter, yet.
The point is that the paranormal talent isn't something
sophisticated. It's something primitive and universal. Only
humans had forgotten they had it. They came to make a

point of not believing in it, somewhere in prehistory. Only those who could believe like the witches and the ones outside who found themselves immune, used it—because belief can kill as well as save a life."

"Even if you're right," said Jai. "Those back here who didn't believe had no part in building the Mass."

"Yes, they did," said Chaz. "The primitive part of their minds worked in spite of them, to survive. They just couldn't use what they built, until they believed they could."

"So you say," Jai answered. "But if you're wrong, you're going to be killing them by slow suffocation to come, when the rot comes in through those holes you've made and strangles them."

"Only I'm not wrong," said Chaz. "All they have to do is face the rot and believe, to conquer it."

He turned and walked back to the table with the camera and recording equipment. The bulky man came forward to bar his path.

"Let him talk," Jai said behind him. The bulky man moved aside. Chaz reached the equipment.

"Only you don't really know for sure, do you?" continued the voice of Jai.

"I believe," said Chaz. "That's all I ask anyone else to do."

He faced the equipment.

"All right, people of Chicago District," he said into it. "Here we go. Whether we win or lose, here we go; because there's no other direction left for us. Reach out with your minds, join me, and end the rot."

He reached for the Mass on Earth once more. But this time, as he did so, he carried in his mind an image of himself as a seed crystal lowered into a nutrient solution that was the as-yet-unaware minds of the four million people of the Chicago District.

"Come on, damn you!" he said, suddenly furious at them. "Join me, or sit where you are and die when the rot gets to you. It's up to you. You built the Mass—*use it!*"

He stood, waiting. For a long moment it seemed nothing was going to happen; and then, slowly at first, he felt himself being joined. He felt himself growing in otherness and strength . . . knowledge of the Mass waking to consciousness in the innumerable minds about him. The mental seed crystal that was himself was joined by the crystal of other minds, solidifying out of the nutrient subconscious, and their unity was growing . . . faster . . . and faster . . .

"Watch," he said to them all over the equipment, pointing up through the transparent dome overhead at the sullen cloud layer, darkening now toward night and already streaked and stained with red in the west. "This is how we begin to kill off the rot."

He reached for the power of the Mass. But now he was many times multiplied by the minds waking up around him; and the Mass-force responded as something much greater than it had ever been. It came at his summons.

It came as it had come before; and there was nothing that could stand before it. It came like the first man striding upright across the face of his world. It came like the will of a people who would not die, breaking out of the trap into which they had fallen. Chaz had imagined it once as a great, dark mountain of wind—and as a great wind it came.

It blew across the buildings and domes of a sealed city; and the spores of the rot that were touched by it died instantly, as they had died within the lungs of witches and the immune exiles. It gathered strength and roared like a storm. It spun into a vortex, stretching up toward the lowering clouds overhead as the horn of a tornado stretches down toward the Earth. It touched the cloud layer and tore it to tatters, spinning the gray vapor into stuff like thin smoke, then into nothingness.

It ripped apart the sky, moving toward the west, destroying clouds and the rot as it went. A long split opened in the thick cover above the city, stretching westward; and like the thunder of ice going out when spring comes to a long-frozen land; and in that split the sun suddenly blazed clear in a cloudless space above a free horizon.

Below the top floor of the Embry Tower, the mind of Chaz was now wrapped in the crystalline unity that was the consciousness of some millions of other minds, just wakened and waking to their ancient abilities. About him, Chicago breathed newly breeze-stirred air with four million breaths. Not merely Eileen, not merely the witches, or the immunes from outside like Red Rover, or even Jai and the Citadel Mass workers—but all those who lived and were human were now beginning to join the unity, striking back with the non-physical tool they had created when all purely physical tools failed them, at the enemy that had threatened to choke them to death or seal them in air-conditioned tombs.

The last clouds went. The sunset spread across the sky like a cloth of gold. And in the east, like sequins along its fringe, where the gold deepened in color toward the night, glittered and burned the first few beacon lights of the stars, unobscured once more—and now, in real terms, waiting.